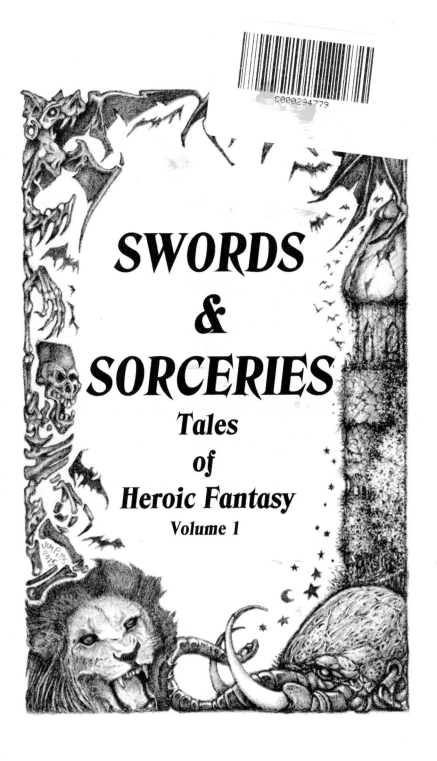

SWORDS
&
SORCERIES
Tales
of
Heroic Fantasy
Volume 1

SWORDS
&
SORCERIES

Tales of Heroic Fantasy
Volume 1
Presented by

David A. Riley
Jim Pitts

PARALLEL UNIVERSE PUBLICATIONS

ISBN: 978-1-9161109-2-2
Parallel Universe Publications, 130 Union Road,
Oswaldtwistle, Lancashire, BB5 3DR, UK

Dedicated to the Memory of writer and editor
Charles Black
who had intended to publish
an anthology like this.

And to the eternal spirit of
Robert E. Howard
who started it all.

CONTENTS

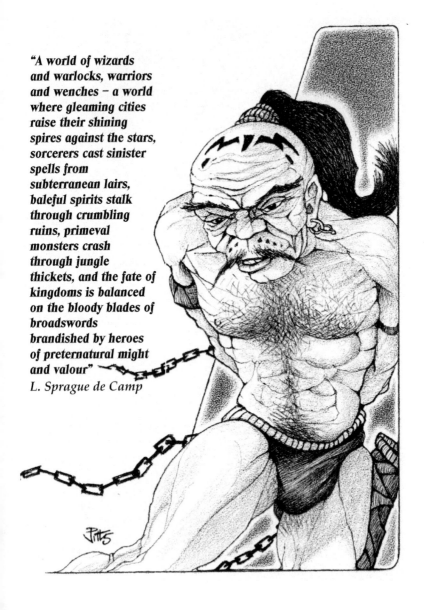

"A world of wizards and warlocks, warriors and wenches – a world where gleaming cities raise their shining spires against the stars, sorcerers cast sinister spells from subterranean lairs, baleful spirits stalk through crumbling ruins, primeval monsters crash through jungle thickets, and the fate of kingdoms is balanced on the bloody blades of broadswords brandished by heroes of preternatural might and valour"

L. Sprague de Camp

INTRODUCTION

It was in 1965, when I came across a copy of L. Sprague de Camp's anthology *The Spell of Seven*, that I first encountered the genre of swords and sorcery. And I couldn't have had a better introduction, with stories by such fantasy luminaries as Fritz Leiber (*Bazaar of the Bizarre*), Clark Ashton Smith (*The Dark Eidolon*), Lord Dunsany (*The Hoard of the Gibbelins*), L. Sprague de Camp (*The Hungry Hercynian*), Michael Moorcock (*Kings in Darkness*), Jack Vance (*Mazirian the*

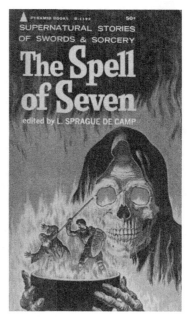

Magician), and last but by no means least, Robert E. Howard (*Shadows in Zamboula*). With its cover by the great Virgil Finlay, this was a ground-breaking and important collection which, not surprisingly, gave me a lifelong love of the genre

The 1960s was a great time for swords and sorcery. Soon publishers like Lancer Books would be reprinting all of the Conan, King Kull, and Bran Mak Morn stories of Robert E.

Howard, and other writers would begin their own careers in the genre like Lin Carter (himself a great editor, responsible for the Ballantine Adult Fantasy series, which brought so many masterpieces of fantasy back into print after decades of neglect). Michael Moorcock would come to dominate the fantasy scene with Elric of Melniboné, Hawkmoon, and The Eternal Champion. Others were Fritz Leiber, whose Fafhrd and Gray Mouser stories added some much-welcomed humour.

I could do no better than use de Camp's own words when he graphically described the genre in his introduction to *The Spell of Seven* with this question:

"How would you like to escape to a world of wizards and warlocks, warriors and wenches – a world where gleaming cities raise their shining spires against the stars, sorcerers cast sinister spells from subterranean lairs, baleful

spirits stalk through crumbling ruins, primeval monsters crash through jungle thickets, and the fate of kingdoms is balanced on the bloody blades of broadswords brandished by heroes of preternatural might and valour?"

If your answer is *Yes* then this book should be right for you.

Today there are new masters of swords and sorcery.

SWORDS & SORCERIES

Under his own Carnelian Press imprint, Steve Dilks is the editor and publisher of two fanzines, *The Hyborian Gazette* and *Twilight Echoes – Tales of swords & dark magic*. His Bohun story featured in this book is the second in an ongoing series set in the time when 'Egypt was still a dream in the eye of Ra, the sun god'. The first, *The Festival of the Bull*, was published in *Swords of Adventure #1*, by Rainfall Books.

Steve has been published in *WeirdBook*, *Startling Stories* and *Savage Scrolls*. His novellas of Gunthar, the Black Wolf of Tatukura, first began appearing as a series of e-books in 2013. Labelled as 'sword-&-sorcery' or 'sword-&-super science' they were collected together with a new story for the paperback omnibus edition, *Gunthar – Warrior of the Lost World*. A recent novella, *Riders of the fire*, is an addition to the post-nuke pulp genre.

Steve Lines is a musician, artist, editor, and occasional writer and runs Rainfall Records & Books with John B. Ford. He lives in England in darkest Wiltshire just a few miles from the Avebury stone circle, Silbury Hill and West Kennett Longbarrow. He has been illustrating books, magazines and fanzines since the mid '70s and has worked for Centipede Press, Lindisfarne Press, Mythos Books, Dark Moon Books and Rainfall Books, amongst others. With John

B. Ford he wrote *The Night Eternal*, a dark Arabian fantasy. He has published three volumes of his music autobiography *From Nowhere to Obscurity* and a book of song lyrics *From Nightmares to Infinity.* He has been in several bands including Storm-clouds, The Tryp, The Chaos Brothers, The Doctor's Pond, and The Ungrateful Dead. He is currently working on a new album by The Ungrateful Dead titled *Dali's Brain,* putting together a new line-up of The Doctor's Pond; editing a book of sketches by Bruce Pennington and generally keeping himself busy.

Susan Murrie Macdonald is a free-lance wordsmith: ghost-writer, blogger, journalist. She has published roughly twenty short stories, mostly fantasy, but also some science fiction, westerns, romance, and children's stories. She is the author of *R Is For Renaissance Faire*, a children's book based on her four years as a volunteer with the Mid-South Renaissance Faire. She is a stroke survivor, although she has been out of the wheelchair almost two years and can limp half a mile with the help of a cane. She is an ex-copy editor and an ex-teacher. She still works as a freelance proof-reader. She is a staff writer for Krypton Radio with over a hundred

articles posted on their website. She is, of course, working on a novel; isn't everyone?

Susan lives in a small town in Tennessee about twenty kilometres from Memphis. She is married to a travel agent and has a son and daughter of university age. She has stories in *Tales from OmniPark*, *Under Western Stars*, *Space Force: Building a Legacy*, *Cat Tails: War Zone*, *Wee Tales*, *The Caterpillar*, *Sirius Science Fiction*, *Itty Bitty Writing Space*, *Bumples*, *Alternative Truths*, *More Alternative Truths*, *Paper Butterfly*, *Sword and Sorceress*, *Knee-High Drummond and the Durango Kid*, *Barbarian Crowns*, and *Supernatural Colorado*.

Geoff Hart writes, "I always loved Fafhrd and the Gray Mouser." His story, *Chain of Command*, is an affectionate homage to Fritz Leiber's disreputable heroes, but "with gender swapped protagonists and a more modern sensibility."

Geoff has published or sold twenty-four stories, including in two of Darrell Schweitzer's Lovecraft anthologies (*Mountains of Madness Revealed* and *Shadows Out of Time*) from PS Publishing, two stories in *Andromeda Spaceways Inflight Magazine*, four stories in the *Tesseracts* anthology series, and stories in *After Dinner Conversations*, *Paper*

Butterfly and *Polar Borealis*. For more information visit him at www.geoff-hart.com.

Gerri Leen lives in Northern Virginia and originally hails from Seattle. In addition to being an avid reader, she's passionate about horse racing, tea, ASMR vids, and creating weird one-pan meals. She has work appearing in *Nature, Galaxy's Edge, Deep Magic, Escape Pod, Daily Science Fiction, Cast of Wonders,* and others. She has edited several anthologies for independent presses, is finishing some longer projects, and is a member of the SFWA and the HWA. See more at gerrileen.com.

Eric Ian Steele is a British screenwriter, novelist, and film director. He is the writer of the thriller feature film *The Student* (2017) made in Hollywood by The

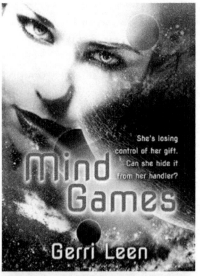

Cartel (Stephen King's *Creepshow*) and the sci-fi action feature film *Clone Hunter* (2012). He is an Amazon Top 100 novelist and the author of two horror novels – the sci-fi/horror story *Experiment 9* and the urban werewolf novel *The Autumn Man*, as well as the short story collection *Nightscape*, published by Parallel Universe Publications in hardcover, paperback and e-book. His short stories can be found in numerous anthologies and zines. He has just finished directing his first feature film, which he also wrote. It is a British vampire movie set in the world of social care titled *Boy #5*.

Chadwick Ginther is the Prix Aurora Award nominated author of *Graveyard Mind* and the *Thunder Road Trilogy*. His short fiction has appeared in many magazines and anthologies, including *On Spec* and *Abyss & Apex Magazine*, and his story *Cheating the Devil at Solitaire* was recently

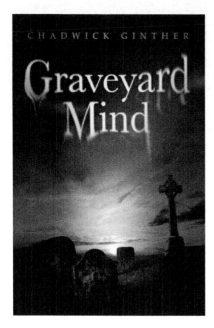

longlisted for the Sunburst Award. His novels *Thunder Road*, *Tombstone Blues* and *Too Far Gone* were published by Raven-stone Books. ChiZine Publications recently published *Graveyard Mind*.

He lives and writes in Winnipeg, Canada, spinning sagas set in the wild spaces of Canada's western wilderness where surely monsters must exist.

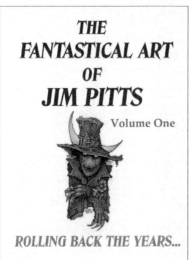

Adrian Cole has been writing stories set in his own fantasy series such as the Voidal and Elfloq for many years, as well as reviving Elak, King of Atlantis, originally created by the late Henry Kuttner. Adrian's first collection of Elak tales was recently published by Pulp Hero Press to much acclaim. Though not sword and sorcery, his collection *Nick Nightmare Investigates* won the 2015 British Fantasy Award for best collection and he is a regular contributor to *Weirdbook* magazine, as well as having stories in anthologies such as *Year's Best Fantasy, Year's Best Fantasy and Horror, The Mammoth Book of Halloween, Occult Detective Quarterly Presents,* and *The Alchemy Press Book of Horror.*

And, of course, there is Jim Pitts, whose illustrations add so much to the interior as well as the covers of this book. Jim's career goes back to the 1970s when he created artwork for David Sutton's fanzine *Shadow*. Since then he has contributed artwork to a wide variety of publications. A hardback retrospective of Jim's work was published in 2017, *The Fantastical Art of Jim Pitts*. This was divided into two volumes for the soft cover version, which included a number of new pieces.

These are the contributors in the first of our planned swords and sorcery anthologies. It's an idea that started over a year and a half ago at the funeral of writer and editor Charles Black, where it was that I learned for the first time that he had always intended to publish a series like this, but worsening health and his untimely death prevented him. For that reason, I am dedicating this book to Charles. Without his inspiration it would have never happened.

David A. Riley
Oswaldtwistle. 2020

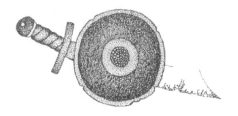

THE MIRROR OF TORJAN SÚL
Steve Lines

The Arid Plains east of the great inland sea of Jorand Zal once held great palaces and beautiful gardens, marvellous and exquisite and the wonder of all Varakash. Now naught but ruins remain. Shattered remnants of once proud dwellings where now only the bat and the *slith* hold sway. The twin moons of Zandor, Hailoph and Jurilium, cast their crimson and emerald rays upon these ancient ruins and on the strange tableau that was unfolding below.

The furtive figure of a man scuttled between the toppled columns and fallen archways of the sprawling necropolis men called Shioth Larr, but unknown to him another figure, equally clandestine, followed silently in his wake.

Phaol Zamh was the first figure. Clad in hardwearing slippers of dark animal fur (the ebon pelt of the *vastoon*) and equally dark robes of black linen, he moved cautiously through the dying and half-decayed cypresses and the shattered mausoleums of the rotting necropolis, his bright, rodent-like eyes casting this way and that in obvious quest for some expected building or landmark.

The second figure wore naught but its own pelt, which was rank and matted with the detritus of the tomb, and crept as stealthily as Phaol Zamh on silent, padded paws. It was a ghoul, and the scent of warm man-flesh had roused it from fitful slumber amid the charnel filth and it now followed its quarry with a ravenous gleam in its dirty amber eyes.

Unfortunately for Phaol Zamh, the ghoul, with the innate cunning of its breed, was downwind of him, lest he would have scented its foul stench in an instant.

Phaol Zamh, still unaware of his stealthy companion, paused and scratched at his untidy beard, smiling to himself as saw ahead of him, at the far end of a long avenue lined with crumbling statues and monuments, a temple. Its domed roof shone strangely in the glare of the moons and seemed to writhe and twist in their spectral light. A wide flight of steps rose from the street to terminate at a massive archway set into the temple wall, which, Phaol Zamh mused, must have been magnificent in its day. The oaken doors were no more, having rotted away aeons ago and within Phaol Zamh could only perceive darkness. He knew that this was the edifice he had traversed half the continent of Varakash to find: the temple of Torjan Súl.

Arriving presently at the foot of the wide stairway, Phaol Zamh paused and his thoughts turned to the events that had led to this current state of affairs.

*

Morphal the necromancer ruled in Shiam. The baleful shadow of his influence stretched long and dark over the lands of Yalór and his eldritch power was feared by all who dwelt in the southern realms of Varakash. From his slim tower of basalt and obsidian he looked out over his realm; but he was troubled.

Shiam was builded upon a lofty peninsula that thrust out northwards into the Straits of Zinnabar. This narrow channel was the sole trade route from the Topaz Sea into the inner sea, the Jorand Zal, and all the rich cities that sat upon its shores. Whilst Morphal ruled the lands of Yalór with his vile necromancies and strange sorceries, the Straits of Zinnabar was a contested domain, for there was one who stood against him.

Across the straits, visible from his tower, Morphal could distantly discern the city of Oaúm, which also stood upon the towering cliffs of a peninsula. Within this city, which thrusted south into the straits, was the demesne of the necromancer Yommoth Queeg, who equally held sway over the lands of Cassilon, to the north. A stalemate existed between the two necromancers and neither possessed the advantage or inclination to wage a wizardly war 'gainst the other.

So it was that an uneasy truce existed between the two.

Now, Morphal had extended his life unnaturally through strange thaumaturgies and incantations which he had torn from the mouldering lips of reanimated liches and cadavers and for three hundred years he had yearned to destroy his rival – who also enjoyed a life stretched unnaturally thin by cunning sorcery.

It had come to the attention of Morphal, while questioning a long-dead concubine as the two lay abed, that there existed an item that could be of service to him. It was rumoured, so the rotting whore had whispered, that lost deep in the crumbling necropolis of Shioth Larr there lay the fabled mirror of Torjan Súl, called the Mirror of Truth. It was said, so the decomposing whore had whispered lovingly into Morphal's attentive ear, that he who gazed into the dark glass of the mirror gazed upon naked truth and such visions of fidelity were, so spake the putrid demimondaine, oft veracious presentments of the future.

It occurred to Morphal that such a device would be most beneficial in discovering spies and infiltrators within his realm. For, he reasoned, he had over fifteen such within the courts of Yommoth Queeg, so it seemed judicious to assume that the converse was also true and most assuredly several of his trusted underlings were doubtless perfidious and in the service of his arch-rival.

Thus it was he called Phaol Zamh, his faithful apprentice to his chambers.

*

A sharp crack of splintering bone brought Phaol Zamh quickly back to awareness of his present surroundings. He turned swiftly to discover the source of the unexpected sound and beheld the slavering ghoul loping towards him. The creature had stepped upon a femur, cracking the bone and appraising Phaol Zamh of its proximity. Thus, the creature howled in rage and frustration and threw itself at the thief. As the malodorous creature lunged at him, Phaol Zamh deftly sidestepped and, as it slipped past, even now turning to attack again - for the reflexes of ghouls were extraordinarily quick - Phaol Zamh produced a pinch of blue powder from a pocket in his sable robe and with a mighty puff, blew it into the muzzle of the ghoul. In an instant the creature fell to the ground, stone dead and Phaol Zamh applauded himself for the foresight he had displayed in bringing a vial of Blue Hibiscus Dust for this very eventuality.

It seemed the long hours of laborious apprenticeship he'd spent at the feet of his master Morphal had garnered fruit, even though it seemed to Phaol Zamh that the necromancer's lessons had lacked the vim and vigour he associated with necromancy, to wit the sorcerous reanimations of gelid corpses. True he had learned divers spells and incantations, but most were not much more than parlour tricks to beguile ignorant servants. When, he had wondered bitterly, would he be given the opportunity to study the ancient tomes and grimoires of Zandor's long dead necromancers and magicians? He had ambitions to become a mage of great potency, but his patience with Morphal was wearing thin.

He had toyed with the notion of joining the service of Yommoth Queeg across the strand, and would have done so were it not for the fact that said personage would doubtless have regarded him a spy of Morphal and slain him, after torturing him hideously and subtly, the which to gain knowledge of Morphal and his intentions.

Giving the dead ghoul no further thought, Phaol Zamh collected his thoughts and gazed up at the ruined temple and the strange dome of shifting shadow. Slowly he began to ascend the sweeping staircase toward the dark portal before him.

With acute trepidation he entered the dark, musty chamber. All was in ruins. The ancient furnishings and accoutrements had long crumbled to dust and friable wood and a patina of grime lay upon everything.

Of a sudden Phaol Zamh was startled by a breeze that swept up an eddy of dust that began to whirl and twist in a writhing column. *Was this the mighty sorcerer Torjan Súl himself, coalescing from the detritus of ages?* He stood ready, sword drawn, knowing that neither his blade, nor his rudimentary necromancy would avail him aught 'gainst the mightiest necromancer of Varakash, but within moments the dancing motes subsided and fell slowly to the floor.

'Twas but a breeze, thought Phaol Zamh to himself. *But I must be most cautious, for there must, of a surety, be some sorcerous entrapments proximate to the mirror I seek.*

Thrusting his blade back into its scabbard, Phaol Zamh

strode carefully but purposefully across the debris-strewn chamber to another ascending staircase that his keen eyes had discerned at the far end of the room.

He had but momentarily placed his boot on the first step of the staircase when the attack came. Something black descended upon him from the lofty shadows. Quick it was and dangerous. Phaol Zamh felt blood on his cheek as his flesh was torn by sharp talons. Swiftly his blade was free and he stepped back to see what manner of creature had attacked him. Looking up it seemed as though the very shadows themselves were descending upon him in a fluttering swarm as dark forms fell from the cobwebbed arches high above. Again one swooped towards him.

"Bats!" he cried.

He ducked the attack of the second creature, which was about the size of a Zukandan fruit bat, but these were not eaters of fruit he knew – they were vampires and it was warm blood they craved. *His!*

Phaol Zamh stepped back into the chamber as the swarm of voracious bats flittered about him.

"Who dies first, vampire demons?" he screamed and began to whirl his blade in a swirling pattern of silvered death. As the furred creatures flew at him they met his blade and fell, cut to pieces, to flutter and flop uselessly upon the flagstones. Occasionally one would penetrate his web of death and inflict upon him a painful slash with teeth or talon, but in the main the creatures were no match for his swordsmanship.

After battling thus for some minutes Phaol Zamh began to wonder how long he could sustain his defence, for the assault of the bats seemed unending, but even as this thought occurred to him the attack ceased, almost as swiftly as it had begun. Suddenly he was alone as the last of the creatures flitted back up into the shifting shadows. About him lay a carpet of twitching corpses. Picking one up, he wiped the putrid blood from his blade using its leathery wings and once again turned towards the staircase.

Torn and bloody; a myriad scratches and shallow cuts crisscrossing his face and arms, Phaol Zamh slowly ascended the sweeping staircase, his one hand upon the grime encrusted balustrade for purchase, the other upon the hilt of his sword. As he climbed in the uncertain light it seemed that shadows skulked behind him, following him up the stairway like sentient liquid. Shaking his head to clear it of these childish fancies Phaol Zamh looked to the upper ceiling, ever wary of another attack by the vicious bats.

Presently he saw that he had arrived at another vast chamber which had for its ceiling the domed roof he had observed from without. But, other than its analogous dimension, it was in no wise comparable to the room he had just quitted. The chamber was appointed in a most luxurious manner. Thick carpets lay strewn about the floor; velvet hangings and magnificent tapestries cloaked the walls; furniture, most delicately carved from ebony, ivory, jet, amber and jade was arranged about the room and these divans, chairs and couches were covered in the skins and hides of extinct creatures and cushions and bolsters of silk and satin lay strewn upon them.

But all these magnificent items were as nothing when compared with the creature that reclined upon a large divan in the centre of the chamber, for there reposed a woman of incredible beauty. Midnight coloured silks clung to her body, flowing over voluptuous breasts and hips and clinging seductively to firm, rounded buttocks like the passionate caresses of an attentive lover. Her eyes were red as blood and her long black hair was coiled about her pallid face in dark tendrils and fell past her shoulders in tumbling cascades dark as a demon's heart. She smiled with sensuous, ruby coloured lips, moistening them with her small, pointed tongue, and spoke:

"Welcome Phaol Zamh to the chambers of Ereshkiga, the Queen of Shadows."

Her voice was as sweet as honeyed almonds and as she spoke she gestured languidly with an exquisite hand for Phaol Zamh to sit beside her upon the divan. Despite his misgivings and his innate mistrust of the beautiful creature, Phaol Zamh found, much to his surprise, that he meekly walked towards the divan and sat himself beside the enchanting creature.

As he sat his eyes turned to a small object draped with a silken cloth that stood at about waist height adjacent to the divan. Ereshkiga noticed the direction of his gaze and a sly smile slowly spread across her pallid features. Her small, pointed tongue flicked out and moistened her voluptuous lips luscious ripe as pomegranates.

"You are indeed a rarity Phaol Zamh for there are very few who manage to gain egress to my inner sanctum. You must indeed be a warrior and conjurer of some potency and strength."

Unsettled, Phaol Zamh found himself unable to answer, for the seductive beauty of Ereshkiga near to overwhelmed him. Her scent was heady and heavy and as intoxicating as the pollen of the Yellow Lotus.

Ereshkiga continued: "There have been many before you, brave, intrepid souls all, but most have fallen foul of the ghouls in the ruins without, or the ever-thirsting bats of my domain, or the myriad other haunters of this dark metropolis. But know this Phaol Zamh – all had two things in common – all sought the Mirror of Torjan Súl and all died."

Mocking humour shone within her unsettling crimson eyes as Phaol Zamh realised that this creature knew of his quest and it seemed that he was but a plaything with which she was toying for her own malicious amusement. He wondered how long it would be before she tired of her game and slew him. Furiously he fought against the lassitude that held him and opened his mouth to deny her claim but Ereshkiga spoke first.

"Do not trouble me with your pathetic lies thief for my shadow creatures tell me all." There was a curious half-suppressed gloating expression lurking within her crimson eyes that made Phaol Zamh uneasy, but her power over him was most potent.

As Phaol Zamh fell under the spell of the radiant creature of darkness he discerned dark shadows drifting across the carpets, seeming to creep stealthily from the darkened areas of the chamber but could see no objects by which they may have been cast. Vague sounds of whispering reached his ears also coming from the regions of gloom and also it seemed from the vast dome high above where all was in deep shadow.

Ereshkiga glanced at the shadows that thronged and roiled with a curious disquiet at the dim extremities of the chamber.

"They cannot cause you hurt unless I will it, Phaol Zamh," said Ereshkiga, "they are the Shadowkind and I their Queen."

Phaol Zamh fought with all the strength of will he could muster against the intoxicating influence of Ereshkiga, his mind summoning weird incantations and mantras to aid in his defence. Slowly, oh so slowly, he could feel the soporific lassitude dissipating, but at what cost. It was draining his strength most rapidly and he was already nigh unto exhaustion.

"There have been few souls who have ventured as far as you have, intrepid Phaol Zamh, you are indeed a warrior of great strength and fortitude and for this I am most pleased. The lure of the mirror ever draws the moths to the flame and only the strongest survive to sit beside me on my divan.

As he fought the invisible bonds that entrapped him a part of Phaol Zamh's mind wondered just what the Queen of Shadows gained from prolonging his life. Why did she not just slay him?

"You wonder why I have not allowed my pets to devour you Phaol Zamh?"

The apprentice started in fearful surprise – Ereshkiga could read his mind? No, it was a logical conclusion to make – at least he hoped so.

"Do not be so eager to hurry your demise my fluttering moth." So saying the Queen of Shadows exerted the full potency of her will upon Phaol Zamh, but the apprentice wizard fought back with one last valiant attempt to break free, his failing will clashing with hers in violent struggle. For a moment Phaol Zamh beheld a look of annoyed anger deep within the eyes of Ereshkiga and at the same moment he felt her will recede and once again her words were as almonds dipped in honey.

"You are strong Phaol Zamh. There a few who can withstand Ereshkiga, the Shadowqueen."

Phaol Zamh said nothing for he knew how close he had come to being overpowered by the dark will of the demon-queen. He had been but moments away from breaking and knew he could not withstand another such battle of wills. Ereshkiga continued in a sultry voice laden with innuendo:

"Yes, you are strong indeed... so strong, but you are yet a man and I... a... woman." As she spoke she moved closer to the wizard-thief caressing his neck with the long, elegant fingers of her right hand. Her touch was as cold as the desert night but Phaol Zamh found it strangely erotic and despite himself he shivered with pleasurable anticipation. As Ereshkiga had moved to fondle him the silks she wore had moved across her bare flesh most erotically exposing the luscious swell of her ripe breasts and revealing much of her exquisite body. Phaol Zamh felt himself sliding into a torpid state of ecstasy as he succumbed to the ministrations of the sensual and beautiful creature beside him.

It seemed to Phaol Zamh that he was sinking deep into a velvet sea of pleasure. He closed his eyes as his whole body tingled and vibrated with overpowering lust and he felt his blood, warm and strong, pulsing madly in his veins. A flicker of triumph shone deep within the crimson eyes of the Shadowqueen, unnoticed by Phaol Zamh, and, a brief smile of satisfaction touched her lips as the wizard-thief fell under her baleful influence. She moved her face towards his and began to nuzzle seductively at his neck. Phaol Zamh felt the delicious caress of her probing tongue as it licked the sweat from his flesh and then the burning hot kiss of her lustful lips as they kissed his throat.

Moaning with pleasure and sinking even deeper into a torpid state of sensual lassitude Phaol Zamh opened his eyes for the briefest instant. At the same moment Ereshkiga moved her head away from his neck, secure in the knowledge that Phaol Zamh was hers. Momentarily their eyes met. Instantly her intoxicating spell was shattered, for Phaol Zamh glimpsed nothing within those burning crimson eyes save a soulless emptiness and a ravening hunger. With another supreme effort of will he shattered the shackles of his lethargy and pushed the vile female away.

Ereshkiga gave an enraged scream and lunged at the thief, her face the visage of an enraged demon, her crimson eyes glaring with lust, hate and hunger. Sharp fangs gleamed in the light and her voluptuous lips were stained with blood.

His blood!

"Vampire!" screamed Phaol Zamh and, jumping to his feet, he drew his scimitar and in one swift movement slashed at the approaching creature. The strong Tarkan blade cut cleanly through the left forearm of the vampire as she reached for his throat and the limb fell bloodless to the floor, writhing and twisting like some enraged serpent. Phaol Zamh watched in dismayed horror as it then flew from the floor and re-attached itself to the stump from which it had been severed. There was a melding of flesh and bone and the limb was restored.

"Fool, you can't kill that which is undead!"

Phaol Zamh said nothing.

"Now, you die!" So saying Ereshkiga raised her hands towards the shadowed ceiling and screamed "Now my children, now!"

Phaol Zamh spared a quick glance upwards and saw that pieces of darkness were beginning to detach themselves from the ebon dome and flutter towards him.

"Your bats have tasted my blade once already witch-queen and it shall be my blade that drinks blood this day.

So saying Phaol Zamh planted his feet firmly and flourished his scimitar, awaiting the attack of the bats. Laughter filled the room as Ereshkiga mocked him. "My children are no bats wizardling. They are the Shadowkind."

With that Phaol Zamh felt himself smothered as something resembling a lich shroud fell upon his face. Where it touched his flesh burned like fire. Tearing it from him he made to throw it across the chamber but watched in horror as it flapped like an insubstantial wind-tossed blanket upon the air and arrowed back at him. Shadow! It was shadow! Somehow sentient, somehow substantial, but shadow. Bringing up his blade he sliced through another of the sorcerous things flapping towards him. His blade ripped through it like it was rotten linen, but the thing did not die (if indeed it lived!) – nor did it bleed, rather the two pieces of ebon night reassembled and attacked once again with renewed vigour.

Behind him he heard the cackling laughter of Ereshkiga as she mocked him "That's right, wizardling, you cannot slay a shadow either. My pets will leech your strength and I shall drink deep of your blood before I devour your soul."

The Shadowkind were all around him now. Desperately he parried with his blade, feinting and thrusting in a whirling web of death. Occasionally a flittering shadow would be slashed by his spinning blade, but the pieces would fly beyond his reach to reassemble.

He knew he was doomed, for he could not long maintain his defence against the flapping Shadowkind. The battle must be ended!

Quick as thought Phaol Zamh whirled around to face Ereshkiga, who still stood nearby mocking and gloating as she watched his futile battle. With a mighty sweep of his scimitar he cut into her neck, slicing her head from her body in one blow. The head screamed in agony and rage as it fell tumbling to the floor, black hair spilling around it as it rolled across the carpets. The torso still stood and again no blood issued forth from head or body. Swaying slightly the headless body of Ereshkiga began to move toward him, taloned hands outstretched. Meanwhile the flitting Shadowkind flew widdershins about the tableau, but none attacked.

Phaol Zamh heard a mad, cackling laughter and glancing at the head from which it issued, realised with horror that it was rolling towards the approaching torso in an effort to rejoin it.

In one swift action he moved toward the staggering body and plunged the point of his blade deep into the vile heart of the demon-queen

"No!"

There was a soul-searing scream of agony from the severed head and Phaol Zamh watched in horrible fascination as both head and body swiftly crumbled to fine ash leaving naught but dust upon the floor and the echo of Ereshkiga's final scream in the air. With the vile queen's final exhalation, the Shadowkind fell to the floor as one, like so many dirty rags, and like the snows of spring, melted away to pools of greasy darkness. These then quickly evaporated into clouds of billowing grey mist that swiftly faded.

Phaol Zamh stood, sword at his side, breathing deeply and praised the Gods for the vampire's vulnerability to wood and his foresight in acquiring a Tarkan blade for this adventuring. For only Tarkan blades were fashioned from the steel hard wood of the *tark* trees of Varakash.

His eyes found the silk-covered mirror, the object of his quest. Sheathing his sword, he walked over to stand before it. For a moment he stood, savouring his victory, and then pulled the tapestry away from his prize, coughing at the cloud of dust this action created.

He stood and gazed into the ebon depths of the mirror of Torjan Súl!

If he had expected some vision of momentous import or future revelation, Phaol Zamh was to be disappointed, for staring back at him was his reflection. On closer inspection he noticed that the background was not the chamber in which he stood, but the inner sanctum of Morphal and he noted too, with some puzzlement, that he wore the robes of the great necromancer. Then it was that his cunning and facile mind divined the true nature of the Mirror of Torjan Sul and knew that he must present it to his master forthwith…

*

Morphal the necromancer stepped back from his scrying globe. With a simple gesture he opened the huge ebon doors of his sanctum just as the figure of Phaol Zamh entered clutching a bulky item, wrapped in silk, under his arm.

"Ah," said the necromancer without preamble, "you have it?" This was a rhetorical question for he had observed the adventures of Phaol Zamh most closely by means of his scrying globe, although, to his frustration he had not been able to discern what it was the thief had beheld in the depths of the mirror.

"Yes, most omnipotent master, I have it."

Morphal gripped his gnarled staff tightly with excitement, but sought to conceal his anticipation from his apprentice, for it was not seemly that he been seen to exhibit weakness in the presence of an underling. He gestured to an alcove, "Place it there if you will."

Phaol Zamh carried the mirror over to the alcove indicated and set it upon its carven frame upon the sturdy table that stood there. He took care to ensure the silken wrapping remained in place. Then he stood back.

Morphal did not observe the flicker of anticipation in Phaol Zamh's eyes, for all his attention was focussed upon the object of his desire, the Mirror of Torjan Súl.

Walking towards the table Morphal stopped in front of the concealed mirror and reached out his gnarled left hand to clasp the silk. With an extravagant flourish he pulled the covering from the mirror and stared deep within the dark depths of the glass. For moments Morphal stood there silent, evidently transfixed by the tableaux revealed to him

Phaol Zamh crept stealthily nearer the necromancer until he could see what it was that Morphal descried within the swirling depths of the glass.

The thief saw with utter dismay that the mirror displayed naught but the true and concise reflection of the necromancer.

Had his conjecture at the properties of the mirror been incorrect?

But then movement within the smoky glass caught his eye. The image of the necromancer began to age most rapidly, the skin of his face stretching and thinning until it began to fall away from the skull in a snowstorm of desiccated flakes. There was a tortured scream of anguish from the necromancer and Phaol Zamh turned his eyes to see that Morphal was in reality decaying just as displayed within the mirror. Phaol Zamh's eyes flashed with triumph. The necromancer thrashed and flailed in agony as his body swiftly decomposed. His features were now that of a skull but from the dark sockets there still stared the glaring eyes of the mage and these were fixed upon Phaol Zamh in rage and hatred. Skeletal hands vainly tried to perform gestures of magical import and a mouth that had no lips or tongue made futile attempts to articulate incantations. Phaol Zamh laughed in triumph as the body of the sorcerer fell to the floor, a heap of grey dust and sorcerous robes. Morphal was dead.

Phaol Zamh stooped and picked up the raiment of Morphal, shaking it vigorously until all vestiges of the decayed sorcerer had fallen free. With a flourish as theatrical as that of his dead master he donned his robes. Then he summoned an underling and commanded that the mirror be presented to Yommoth Queeg, as a gift from the new necromancer of Yalór.

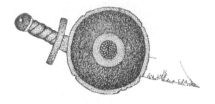

THE HORROR FROM THE STARS
Steve Dilks

1

Bohun of Damzullah rolled and came to his feet in the sand, his curved scimitar flashing before him in the desert sun. He crouched low, eyes narrowed against the stinging grit of the sand storm that sought to flay the flesh from his exposed face. His desert robes whipped wildly, and it was all he could do to keep his sandaled feet braced in the moving drifts. A muffled growl in front of him alerted him to the danger he still faced. He tensed, head hung between mighty shoulders, gripping the hilt of his sword in a hammered fist as he raised the spiked shield before him with his left arm. Staring over its rim, he could see virtually nothing, only streaks of sunlight, through the whirling dervish that was the desert storm.

Then it was upon him. He saw the red gleaming eyes, the curved flashing fangs as the giant hyena launched itself to the attack. It came in like a cyclone and, throwing himself down on one knee, Bohun raised his shield while his steel slashed out in a mighty arc. He was rewarded with a howl then the beast had ploughed into him, knocking him to the ground. It yelped as it rolled past him into the storm. He dared not turn and press the advantage for he knew that its companion would be on his back in seconds. Again he came to his feet. The second beast came in low, slavering jaws opened wide. Bohun swung his shield, slamming the edge hard into those snapping fangs. They bit down and he felt the steel crumple like parchment paper. His curved steel flashed again and blood sprayed as the beast's head was half severed from its neck. Its howls were lost in the winds of the storm. Flinging the mangled buckler aside, the giant black wheeled. He could see the first hyena stood braced in the sand, red eyes blazing, head hung between thick set shoulders which came up to his chest. Thick black hair bristled along its flanks as drooling lips drew back into a hideous snarl. A manic cry that sounded like laughter burst from its throat and then it loped forward, crossing the space between them like a juggernaut of death. Bohun crouched in the drifts with both hands on the hilt. At the last moment he dived to his left and as the beast passed him, jaws snapping, he twisted, chopping at the hyena's hindquarters. It yelped as its back leg gave way, the tendons severed. As it collapsed he reversed his hands on the hilt and, rearing up, brought the scimitar down, ramming the point deep into its flank. He threw his whole weight down on the pommel until he fell to his knees in the sand, the blade drinking deep of the beast's heart. It barked out its life, twitching in defiance of its own demise. Then, finally, its struggles ceased altogether, its eyes glazing as its jaws spread wide in a grimace of death.

Panting, he leaned on the sword for a moment, bending his head to keep the gritting sting of sand from his eyes. Then, as suddenly as it had sprung up, the storm passed, and clean sunlight beat down fiercely from the blue vaulted sky. Rising to his feet, the giant black from Damzullah set a sandaled foot on the beast's carcass and wrenched his sword free. Wiping the blood on its mangy fur, he slammed the blade back into its scabbard and stood frowning with one hand resting on the pommel.

His horse was dead, half buried in the drifts, its throat torn out by the beasts when they had attacked. He had not seen them until it was too late. One minute the sky was clear and the next it had darkened ominously. The sands had risen as if by some malevolent hand and with it, out of the storm, the hyenas had come. They were like wraiths; ghost spirits of the underworld come to wreak vengeance on the living from some hellish domain.

Despite the heat, a chill touched the giant warrior's spine and he rolled his shoulders. With a grunt, he trudged his way back over to where his mount lay and began loosening his supplies. He looked down on the animal with regret. A magnificent black stallion, it had served him well these past few weeks.

At least it had been a quick death, he thought grimly. He slung the gilt worked saddle over one shoulder and, rising, let the saddle bags hang down loosely over his bull like neck. In the distance, he could see the whitewashed walls of his destination, Ibn-Shahk, shimmering in the heat waves. He took a measured swig of water from his canteen and screwed the cap back on slowly. All the while he stared through flint hard eyes at the minarets and green domes of that distant city.

He began to walk.

2

"And because you lost your horse you think we should let you in?" The swarthy, hook nosed guard thrust his head forward, disdain written on his face as his companion looked over with equal contempt. Dressed in desert robes, they leaned arrogantly on their long-bladed pikes. At their sides were curved sabres in lacquered scabbards. Bohun stood between them under the shaded arch of the gateway. He said nothing but stood rooted to the spot. The saddle over his shoulder weighed heavily and he was quickly tiring of their games. Behind him, people were waiting to enter the city gates. Ahead, he could see the palms and fountains that lined the dusty streets, the carts with their oxen and the sellers crying from open canopied stalls the delights of their wares. But it was not these sights that tried the patience of the ebon skinned giant from Damzullah. It was the thought of the woman he loved hidden somewhere deep within these walls... At last his anger flared and a hand snatched out toward the guard's throat. He gripped it and pulled the man in close. As the second guard moved forward, Bohun let slip the saddle from his shoulder. It landed heavily on the man's feet and the sentry tripped into the dust, cursing. His plight was greeted by howls of laughter from the merchants and cattle herders sweating in the sun.

"Dog!" snarled Bohun, pulling the man he held in close. "Have I not already told you that I bear the seal of the sultan?" He snatched a tubed scroll from his robes and waved it before the guard's bulging eyes. The man gagged, clutching desperately at the iron hand wrapped around his throat. The toes of his sandals kicked out as he was lifted from his feet. Bohun shook him before throwing him back against the wall. He slid to the ground in a dishevelled heap, retching in the dust. The other sentry scrabbled back, limping over to where a small hammer hung next to a gong by the wall. Bohun's hand reached for his sword hilt.

"As you value your life, cur, do not sound that gong."

The guard hesitated and the crowd gathered behind Bohun went suddenly quiet.

"By T'agulla! I've had a bellyful this day. First my horse gets killed by hyenas and now you would insult me by denying me entry into your city. Well, I'll—"

"Make way, citizens. I think I can be of assistance here."

Bohun looked over his shoulder. He saw a man in peasant's garb shouldering his way through the throng. He was a westerner, pale skinned with close-cropped hair and frank blue eyes. He came up to stand before the giant Damzullahan.

"Please, stranger. No need to unsheathe your sword. Allow me."

Curious as to the man's actions, Bohun shrugged and let his hand fall away from his sword hilt. The man turned to the guards and spread his hands. "Good Bahti, good Avam, is this the way we treat honoured guests of the sultan? Here is a man who has papers and a seal to prove it. Come, let us all be friends and forget this nonsense ever happened, eh?"

The crowd murmured agreement and the two sentries looked bashfully from them to the young man again. Begrudgingly, the first guard stepped back and began silently waving them through. Bohun reached down and, lifting his saddle, shouldered it with ease. As he walked through the gate both guards avoided his gaze. Emerging out into the sunlight of the plaza on the other side, he found the man who had intervened standing beside him.

"Welcome to Ibn-Shahk!" he grinned.

Bohun eyed him shrewdly. He saw that he was tall compared to the indigenous folk of this little eastern city. His smock was a sleeveless grey tunic that showed off impressively wide shoulders and arms. Here was no cattle herder. This was a man well used to the rigours of physical endurance. Setting down his saddle, Bohun folded his arms over his massive chest and stared at him. "And what price do you expect of me for your help back there?"

The young man's smile faded. "None. But you could at

least show some gratitude. My name is Tyrun." He outthrust a hand. Hesitantly, the ebon giant extended his own and gripped it. "Bohun." Tyrun's smile reignited and he motioned with his head. "Come then, Bohun of the dour face! I wager you're thirsty from all your adventures. I know where we can get wine and bread."

3

They came to an incongruous looking place, little more than a niche set in a back-street alley and disguised by a red curtain. Nodding to the other patrons, Tyrun motioned Bohun to a low table where they sat on a rug between cushions strewn on the floor. The establishment was low ceilinged, dimly lit and stank of incense and the odour of sweaty men. But to Bohun, after a long day's ride under the burning desert sun, the den was like a breath of fresh spring winds. Wine was brought in a pitcher along with bread, figs and dates. When they had eaten, Tyrun reached for the battered brass pitcher and poured into wooden goblets. A sour red, it soothed Bohun's palate that had subsisted on nothing but water these past few weeks. As his head lightened, so did his mood. He wiped a drape sleeved arm over his lips then looked to his companion.

"I thought these people frowned on the pleasures of the grape."

"They do." He looked around then leaned forward. "At least, in public. But I've not met a desert warrior yet that doesn't pray four times a day and then, at the end of it, swig like a Dionyssian from an open wine skin! These places are kept out of the public scrutiny. Officially, they are for foreigners. But we all know the truth." He waved a hand dismissively.

"You know much. You even have the ear of the guards. How did you end up in this place?"

Tyrun sipped thoughtfully before lowering his goblet. He smiled and there was a hint of something distant reflected in his pale blue eyes.

"I'm a ferryman. I carry people across the River Zallam that flows east of the city. From it, an underground tributary feeds the oasis on which Ibn-Shahk was built. As a child I was taken in a caravan raid and brought here. I was sold as a slave to a merchant. As a teenager I saved his life from men that had a dispute with him. I took a knife thrust that laid me low for quite some time. But I was strong and recovered. The old man passed on two years ago. I found he had not only set me free but had also paid for me to become a full-fledged citizen. In his will he wrote what he called, my 'brave and selfless act in service to the life of his master.' I've remained here ever since."

Bohun nodded. "Fortune favours the brave."

Tyrun shrugged then, with a laugh, swept up his goblet.

"And you, my friend, with the colossal temper. How do you come to the walls of Ibn-Shahk, so far from home?"

Bohun stretched great limbs and leaned forward so that only his companion might hear him. "I come from Damzullah, far to the south."

Tyrun nodded. "I have heard of it."

"There was an uprising. I was exiled then captured and sold as a galley slave. I escaped and made my way back. I learned from some slavers south of Badura that my wife, Dana, was sold to the sultan of Ibn-Shahk. I am here to barter for her freedom. With gold or—" he tapped the hilt of the great curved sword where it lay resting on his lap "—by force if necessary."

Tyrun raised an eyebrow.

"And the scroll you showed the guard at the gate?"

"My bargaining tool." Unconsciously, one hand moved to the parchment concealed under his robes. "I made a deal with those Gharubah slavers I met. They promised this would give me ear to the sultan himself. It is signed by a sheikh of the eastern tribes. I'm to believe his word carries weight here."

"And if it does not?"

Bohun glared, his hand tightening on his sword hilt. "Either she comes with me or I fall here. It is of little consequence." He shrugged massive shoulders and, throwing back his head, drained the last of his wine before reaching for the pitcher again. Tyrun ran a hand through his hair. A smile played on his lips as he regarded the ebon giant dressed in the white desert robes. He shook his head and leaned back with a sigh.

"Sometimes I wish my life were that exciting. I wish you well, warrior. It is no easy thing to be parted from those you love."

Setting down his goblet, Bohun gazed at him.

"I was not jesting when I said fortune favours the brave, Tyrun. A strong youth like you could do well in the world. I've seen the marbled streets of Tharnya. I've beheld the beauty of their women, aye—and I've known their treachery, too. I was taken to that city in chains and those chains were made of gold. By Chaka, I broke them with my bare hands, had them melted down and turned into riches. Soon as I have my wife, I will return there to carve out my fortune."

Tyrun listened thoughtfully, playing with a date between his fingers. "Stirring words. But what of your homeland? Do you not wish to go back there? To end your exile?"

A brooding look came over the giant Damzullahan. He shook his head slowly. "Destiny has other plans for me." He snorted and looked around. "Bah! This is no place for a young man, breaking his back for a handful of coppers. Come with me. With those arms you would soon reap riches in the soft cities of the west."

"The wine has gone to your head, big man."

Bohun stared at the youth for a moment before flashing him a white toothed grin. He laughed and raised his cup in salute.

Just then a woman in yellow silk appeared. She was young and fresh faced with long dark hair. Bohun noticed her slanted mysterious eyes, olive skin and that she was heavy with child.

"Tyrun," she said softly and, at the sound of his name, the young man turned. He stood then, putting his arm around her waist, turned to the Damzullahan.

"Bohun, I would like to introduce you to my wife, Anya. Anya, this is Bohun, from the mighty city of Damzullah. He has important business with the sultan."

Bohun's gaze softened and a faint smile touched his lips. Looking to the youth, he clasped his sword in one hand and rose to his feet with a sigh. "I thank you for what you did for me, Tyrun. I hope your life goes well." He gripped the young man's forearm then bent to shoulder his saddle and belongings.

"Before you part, Bohun... a word of caution." The Damzullahan straightened as Tyrun leaned forward. "All is not well here. Some say the city is under a curse and that the sultan has brought evil to Ibn-Shahk."

"How so?"

The youth glanced around. "It is hard to say. Some months ago, caravan masters came in telling stories of a strange star they had seen falling from the sky. Word of it reached the sultan. He has always been a vain man. He saw it as a personal sign from the gods. He ordered expeditions to find this star and even accompanied them on their searches. Eventually they found it. Or, at least, they found *something*. Since then, things have changed. People began disappearing. First it was just commoners, strangers and the like. Now, none is safe. Daughters have vanished in the night. Some say that Akim Harrad, the sultan himself, is behind it. Whatever awaits you beyond those palace walls, it is best to be on one's guard. Just… beware."

Bohun nodded. "I will heed your words. Know you where I can find lodgings?"

"Try the inns at the crescent quarter as you come out of this street. The rooms are not pretty but you can get supper and a bath for a copper piece."

The Damzullahan nodded his thanks and made for the door.

4

As the sun sank slowly to be extinguished in bands of orange flame, a voice was lifted in prayer from a minaret at the edge of the city. Stars began to blink out, a myriad of frosted jewels dusted across the heavens.

From his second storey tenement window, Bohun leaned against the open frame, his arms folded across his naked chest as he gazed out over the palms and minarets of the little city. His eyes brooded on a structure in the distance. Surrounded by four onion domed towers, it was a flat roofed edifice. The palace of Akim Harrad, the sultan of Ibn-Shahk. No expression crossed the big warrior's face. His countenance may well have been cast from iron, so rigid were his features. Yet, in his eyes was a deep burning light. Even as he stood there, he felt his pulse quicken in anxious expectancy. Tomorrow, he would enter those palace walls and behold his beloved wife for the first time in many moons. Sleep would not come easy to him this night.

But come to him it did and, on the morrow, he rose from the wooden pallet upon which he had slept and donned his mail shirt and robes. Checking his weapons, he buckled his great sword at his waist and, beside it, his curved desert knife. He made sure the scroll he carried was properly housed in its wooden tube before tucking it into his robes. Carrying his saddle and supplies, he came down a wooden stairway that creaked under his weight. The proprietor, a shifty old man dressed in a white cloth wound about his loins, eyed the big Damzullahan as he came down. He sat cross-legged in the entrance way, scratching at lice where they infested his bare body. "Good day, stranger. Will you be wanting another bed for tonight? I can reserve one for a copper piece."

Bohun deliberated. "If you will keep these things safe, old timer, I will be back for them." He lowered his saddle and supplies to the ground. Digging into his pouch, he flicked a coin which the old man plucked deftly out of the air. He gummed the thick edge and cracked a wide smile. "Of course!" he cackled, unlimbering to his feet and padding over to his belongings. "They will be safe here. Any time you want to pick them up, you come." Nodding, Bohun strode into out into the early morning sunlight. He crossed the courtyard and stepped out into the street.

*

As he came up to the palace, the warning Tyrun had given him the evening before was little more than a nagging doubt at the back of his mind. After all, the terrors of a people not his own were of no consequence to him. To heed such superstitions was to invite weakness. And no race was braver, fiercer or mightier than those of Damzullah. They laughed at the fears of other men, all of whom they considered beneath them.

The onion domes of the white walled building reared above him. Reaching the steps, he came up them in easy strides, the soft leather of his sandals slapping the veined marble. Two guards standing to either side of the entrance eyed him warily as he approached. They held long bladed pikes and small gold embossed shields. Over their mail were long sashes of red silk.

"That's far enough, stranger," one growled. "What do you on the steps of the palace of his most glorious magnificence, Akim Harrad? Speak! Or be cut down where you stand."

Bohun halted five steps below them and spread his hands away from his weapons. "I have business with the sultan. In my robes is a letter sealed with his mark from the sheikh of the eastern Gharubah tribes."

"Eastern tribes, eh?" sneered the other guard. Snapping his fingers, he jerked his helmeted head. "Let us see."

Reaching carefully into his robes, Bohun drew out the tube, pulling the scroll out just far enough so they could see the seal. One of the guards gave a surprized grunt. They muttered to each other then called inside the palace. Presently, an extravagantly dressed plump man appeared. He wore a long beard and had dark beady eyes. Those eyes rested on the Damzullahan as the guards related to him what they had seen. He nodded slowly. Smiling at Bohun, he held out his hand.

"May I see the document? I am Vizek, the sultan's chief treasurer."

Bohun eyed him warily. "The document is for the eyes of the sultan. I must be present when he reads it." He had not come so far to be parted from his only hope now. If need be, he would defend the parchment with his life.

"Very well," said Vizek, salaaming. "If you will follow me."

Passing the guards, Bohun stepped into the shadowed corridor of the palace. His eyes had only just adjusted when they came out into a magnificent sweeping hall. The chief treasurer walked ahead of him, his robes swishing out over the inlaid floor. Two guards standing at the hall entrance crossed their long-bladed polearms in front of Bohun as he sought to pass. He stepped back with a snarl, reaching instinctively for his sword hilt. Vizek turned.

"Be not alarmed. I see you are unused to palace etiquette. It is customary to relinquish weapons before being admitted into the presence of the sultan."

Inwardly, Bohun cursed his own eagerness before moving his hand to his sword belt. He did not mention to the treasurer that he had once been captain of the guard to the most powerful ruler of the southern kingdoms. He held out the belt with a nod and it was taken.

Seldom had Bohun seen such opulence. From somewhere music played a dreamlike refrain on a stringed instrument. A peacock in full plumage walked past, pecking at grain that had been strewn on the white marbled floor. Beyond columned archways that ran down the length of the hall, the sound of distant fountains could be heard. Incense filled the air. At the far end of it all sat the sultan himself.

Akim Harrad was a fat, tired looking old man with eyes that shone with dulled mirth from years of extravagant living. Beneath his turban, a grey waving beard reached down to his chest. His robes were of sequined jewels, a rioting clash of colour whenever he moved an arm to pick at a sweet meat from the trays which surrounded him. Nubile slave girls lay all around his high seat, lolling on cushions, tempting him with these delightful dishes. Behind the chair, a slim exotic looking naked girl stood fanning him with slow sweeps of a many feathered fan. Bohun noted that she was a sleek, ebon skinned beauty from the far lands of Khamsu. She eyed the Damzullahan boldly as he strode up before averting her gaze back to the top of the sultan's head. Stood to the other side of the chair was a gigantic black bodyguard stripped to the waist. He wore wide silk pantaloons and gold slippers. His head was cleanly shaven and from one ear dangled a gold hooped earring. His thick arms were folded across his breast and in one hand he held a mighty curved scimitar, much wider and longer than Bohun's own. He flashed Bohun a look of unfeigned hatred before regaining his composure and staring solemnly into space again. He was of the Mungawii and no love was lost between his people and the nation of Damzullah.

They came up to the foot of the dais now and Vizek went to his knees, touching his forehead to the ground. "Your magnificence, a foreigner desires audience. He comes bearing a parchment with your seal from the eastern tribes of the Gharubah."

Bohun stood with legs braced and arms folded. Akim Harrad swept him over with a cool gaze, chewing distractedly on a sweet meat. One hand pushed aside a proffered gold dish and he waved a ringed hand.

"Does he have a name?"

"I am Bohun of Damzullah. Forgive my travel stained appearance. I have ridden hard these past weeks to bring you this." Reaching into his robes he drew out the scroll. The giant bodyguard stepped down and took it, handing it to the sultan before stepping back and taking up his position as before. Akim Harrad opened the container and broke the seal. Unscrolling the papyrus, he sat for some moments reading. Then he rolled it up again and handed it to Vizek.

"Aatami."

The giant bodyguard salaamed. "Yes, your magnificence?"

"In my seraglio there is a young woman from Damzullah. I have just learned that her name is Dana. Bring her to me."

The bodyguard nodded over to two mailed soldiers stood in the shadows of the columns. They departed with a jingle of mail. Bohun's heart hammered in his ribs. Did he think to see a calculating look in the sultan's gaze?

Presently, a red curtain at the side of the hall was thrust open and the two soldiers emerged again. He saw her then — for the first time in many months. From the alcove, across the marbled floor she came, walking between the two guards. As they came up she lowered her head in weary resignation. No longer was she the proud, full-bodied woman he had once loved. Nay: the woman that stood cowering before him now was naked and thin, her hair cropped close to her skull, her back crisscrossed with welts from the kiss of the lash. In her eyes was the downcast look of shame and defeat. *"Dana!"* Her name was torn from his lips. Stumbling across, he knelt on the floor before her and swept her up into his arms. He felt her body stiffen at his touch. His hands felt the welts on her back, the bruises that swelled her limbs, and he bit back a sobbing curse. He knew that months in slavery could change even the hardiest of men. But for a woman it was infinitely worse. In his burning obsession to find her, he had not prepared himself for the reality.

"B-Bohun?"

"I told you I would come."

"Bohun… you must be away," she whispered. "Evil walks here. I have stared into the dark heart of Chaka. It is too late for me… too late. But you must go." She whispered the words as her head bent down to his. He knelt on the floor before her, his arms encircling her waist, his face pressed into her belly. He lifted his head and stared up into her eyes. He saw fear there. Fear and pain. A dark mist descended over his vision and a red rage fired his brain. His hands yearned for a length of steel to lay waste this palace and drench the marbled walls in blood.

"It seems that the sheikh of the eastern tribes holds you in high esteem. It is known that Akim Harrad is a just and merciful man. But, I am afraid, the girl cannot be allowed to leave these walls." said the sultan. "But you are weary. Be our guest and let us feed and bathe you… I insist." He smiled languidly and snapped his fingers. As if at some pre-arranged signal, the guardsman at the hall entranceway drew the doors shut with a hollow boom.

Bohun rose stiffly to his feet. He turned to face the sultan, his hands clenching in murderous rage. He looked into his eyes and saw only coldness there. He noted the ready positions of the guards, the look of sly malice on the face of Vizek, the chief treasurer.

It seemed to Bohun that the end of the trail had come. He had found his love. Now he was prepared to sell their lives as dearly as he could. He did not intend that either of them should survive. This time there would be no taking of captives, no bartering for life over freedom. This time there would only be death.

He laughed; a wild laugh that was the guttural cry of some savage beast.

The guards fell back at the sound and in that moment Bohun struck. He whirled, grasping for the sabre sheathed at the nearest soldier's side. Ripping it from the scabbard he thrust forward, ramming the point through the mailed breast, driving the blade in deep, his shoulder slamming into the man as he bent over, a yard of steel dripping crimson from his back. Wrenching the blade free again, he leaped back as the corpse fell to the floor. The second guard gave a fearful shout even as he drove in with his glaive. It struck Bohun's side, piercing the robes and glancing from the mail shirt beneath. Grunting, the giant black grasped the haft and, dragging the weapon toward him, butted the guard in the face. The man staggered away, his nose a bloody ruin, and the sabre flashed down in a crimson arc, splitting his skull to the teeth. Soldiers came in yelling from the shadows. Dana fell to the floor. Grasping at her husband's thigh, she lowered her head in acceptance of what was to come. With one hand, Bohun ripped the desert robes over his head and hurled them with a laugh into the faces of the approaching guardsmen.

"Now, dogs, you will see how Damzullahans die! Your children's children will remember this day."

He looked across, seeing Akim Harrad staring in disbelief. He saw the giant bodyguard with his scimitar upraised. In that moment he calculated the distance between himself, the sultan, and the soldiers sweeping toward him. He could cut the sultan down and be back to end Dana's life before he himself was overwhelmed. With thought came action. Like a charging lion, Bohun leaped to the dais, steel swinging in his hand. Akim Harrad pressed himself into his chair, eyes wide with terror. Too late, Bohun saw the bodyguard move across and tug at a brocaded rope that hung from the ceiling. Then the ground gave way beneath him and he was sent plunging into darkness below!

5

There was a moment of sickening vertigo then he hit the ground, landing with a cat-like agility into a crouch. He had not fallen far but, as the trap door swung shut above him, he was plunged into darkness. He stood frozen until his eyes became accustomed to the gloom. As his vision slowly adjusted, he noted the glow from a torch bracketed on a wall behind him. From it he could make out a rough estimation of his surroundings. Directly in front of him was a wall and behind a long stone corridor that stretched off into darkness. Raising his sword above him, he could touch the ceiling with the edge but no amount of thrusting could budge the trap through which he had fallen. He did not waste time in trying. Nor did he waste time in useless self-recrimination. Instead, he loped down the corridor on noiseless feet, his eyes flickering into the shadows cast by the guttering torch. That its flame moved so erratically told him that somewhere up ahead was a way out. Suddenly, to his right, he heard a rustle and clink of chain. He froze, his sword raised defensively before him as he twisted into a crouch.

"Who goes there? Show yourself, demon!" a haggard voice cried out.

Bohun's eyes narrowed to slits. He saw an iron grilled cell. Two brown hands clasped at the bars and beyond them he found himself staring into two sunken eyes, mad with terror.

"I am no demon. I am Bohun. Trapped down here as you are."

At the sound of his voice, the wild-eyed prisoner jerked his head. His hair was dirty and unkempt. "Gods! Take your sword, man. Thrust it deep. Strike true. Let not the feeder get me. I beg of you!"

As if for emphasis, he thrust his bony chest up against the bars, his eyes pleading. Bohun shivered then turned away, slinking back into the shadows. A desperate wail followed him as he groped his way out of the torchlight, one hand feeling shakily along the roughhewn wall. Presently, he sensed rather than saw a lessening of the darkness ahead. A draft of clammy air clung about his face. Dimly, he made out a faint grey light. Moving cautiously toward it, he came to a small flight of steps that led up to a solid wooden door. There was a square grille at head height in that door and it was beyond this that the murky light came. He padded up the stair and peered through. As he did, a figure moved in front of the grille and stood facing him.

Vizek!

Instinctively, he drew back but was too late. The treasurer clasped a thin pipe quickly to his lips and blew. A yellowish dust shrouded Bohun's face and his curse ended in a hacking cough. He reeled away and it was as if his legs had suddenly turned to water. He was unconscious before he hit the floor at the bottom of the stair.

*

He came to slowly, groping through the mire of his sluggish dreams. Opening his eyes, he found himself staring into a white marbled chamber. Across from him a gold barred window let in a cool rippling breeze. Outside, he could see the cold glittering stars as they blurred slowly into focus. He grunted and, shaking his head, sought to rise. As he did he realized that his arms were bound tightly behind him. He sat up on a marble divan and swung his legs loosely over the side. Although he had been stripped of his mail, he still wore his breechclout and high strapped sandals. Above him, a gold censer hung from the ceiling. From it drifted the dark misted scent of myrrh and cinnamon. But it was not these sights that stirred the Damzullahan into straining his muscles against his bonds. It was the sight of the figure before him, his face turned casually away as he gazed out into the night beyond the delicate bars of this opulent prison.

"Given time, I know you could break free from the cords that bind you," sighed Akim Harrad. As he spoke, he did not turn but stood gazing out into the night, his hands clasped behind his back. Bohun said nothing. They were alone in the chamber. He spied only one entrance and exit, and that door was barred — *from within.*

Bending his head, he flexed his arms and shoulders until the muscles stood out in great iron ridged bands.

"Did you ever see such a sight?" continued the sultan, his voice barely above a whisper. "The stars… so aloof in the heavens. What worlds beyond them, we wonder? What battles fought out there in the unreachable vastness? What glories to be had? The gods… yes, the gods alone know."

He turned to face the Damzullahan.

"I have touched those glories," Akim Harrad continued, his voice low and intense. His eyes held a fanatical gleam. "I have gazed upon the faces of gods and seen things that would blast your very reason… I have touched both divinity and blasphemy."

"Dog! Where is Dana?"

The sultan spread his hands and gazed at Bohun as if seeing him properly for the first time. "We need her. Savage as she is, she is of nobility. She is strong and her blood line pure."

"Need her for what?" growled Bohun.

Lifting a ringed hand, the sultan stroked his beard. The

Damzullahan's blood ran cold when he saw the thin smile that touched his lips.

"It is beyond your understanding but know this... you too shall witness glory before you die!"

He moved forward then, staring dispassionately. His eyes held a strange light and his lips writhed into a twisted grin. Then, slowly, to Bohun's horror, the sultan's eyes began to roll back, his mouth opening into the semblance of a silent scream. He sank to his knees and threw his head forward. Bohun stared transfixed, the sweat frozen on his naked ebon skin. Akim Harrad's jaws began to widen, elongating impossibly downward. His eyeballs had rolled all the way back into blank white orbs. Something began to bulge in his throat before forcing its way out of his mouth. Long feelers began lashing frantically at the air. Then behind them came something indescribable. A corpse pale body, slimy and gelatinous, like some monstrous insect. It forced itself out of his mouth, oozing down and flopping out onto the marble. Akim Harrad collapsed to the floor. The creature flexed its pale armoured shell and came erect, elongating on stork like appendages. It stood about waist height. Madly lashing feelers whipped in front of it as it began to scuttle ominously in Bohun's direction. Under the shell were row upon row of sharp curving teeth. The whole body was as one gigantic mouth and those teeth opened and closed as if already feasting on human flesh. In that moment, Bohun knew madness. He screamed and broke his bonds with a mighty surge of strength. The cords snapped and he came to his feet just as the thing hurled itself upon him. He caught at the flexing body with both hands and held it away at arm's length though every muscle screamed in violent protest. Twisting his head to one side, he grimaced as feelers whipped wildly at his face and coiled about his torso. More by instinct than design, he swung round, seeking to break the armoured shell of the thing against the marbled dais. He raised its heavy weight above him then brought it slamming down. There was an audible—*crack!* It seemed to clamp on harder, the appendages coiling around his thick thewed arms and neck. Again he sought to break the shell but this time he could not lift the creature high enough to inflict much damage. The feelers had coiled around him with supernatural strength, limiting his range and pulling him ever closer to the gnashing teeth of its mouth.

Straightening, he turned and rammed it hard against the wall. This time the creature made a sound as its shell connected forcefully with the unyielding marble. It gave a loud and urgent high-pitched scream. Gritting his teeth, he drove in again and again. Then he tore back, releasing the grip of one hand and ripping the appendages from around his throat and arm. He struggled free and staggered back into the centre of the chamber.

The thing writhed itself into lashing knots on the floor and, as he stared aghast, he felt something grope at his ankle. It was Akim Harrad. The sultan sought to rise, his hand clutching feebly at Bohun's sandal. His eyes were glazed and a thick white drool dribbled from his lips. "It must feed... let it feed."

Bohun fell back to the wall behind him, horror and loathing knotting a fist deep inside his stomach. The thing had righted itself now and was sending its feelers out along the floor in slithering, undulating waves. It rose up grotesquely and began to walk on its spindly stork like legs. The *clack, clack* was magnified horribly in the room as it advanced slowly into the chamber. Eyes wide with dread, Bohun was barely aware that he had nowhere else to go, that he gripped the wall behind him with outstretched hands.

Then realization dawned upon him and he glanced wildly around. To his right, bracketed high up on the wall, was a torch. Instantly, he ripped it down and leaning forward, waved the flaming object out before him in one hand.

The thing paused then scuttled toward him with preternatural speed. Legs coiled under him, Bohun pushed himself out from the wall and rammed the flaming torch straight into the oncoming mouth. The creature recoiled screaming. It rolled back into a ball along the floor.

"No!" screamed Akim Harrad. He rose feebly and staggered toward the thing.

"Damn you!" snarled the big warrior and swinging up the torch, brought it down with a sweeping blow that caved in his skull. Then Bohun took a hesitant step forward and, licking dry lips, drove the torch down into the creature. It recoiled, spitting and flaming. Then he had leaped up and stamped down viciously again and again until the thing was a broken, jelly-like mush on the floor. Tendrils twitched spasmodically then were still.

Panting, Bohun drew a shaking wrist over his brow. He barely noticed when he let the torch drop to the floor. He stood for a moment shaking with horror then brought his head up sharply. Beyond the chamber, he heard voices raised in alarm followed by running feet and the clink of arms. He looked as fists began banging on the door, remembering that it was locked from the inside. Glancing around, he saw nothing that he could use for a weapon. Knotting his fists, he drew his lips into a thin line and prepared to die.

6

The door crashed in and men spilled into the room with sabres bared. Those first over the threshold fell back from the sight that greeted them. At the centre of the chamber stood Bohun; a gigantic half-naked ebon giant, head lowered, eyes glowering with fists hung low at his sides. They saw the corpse of their sultan and the stiffened remains of something unwholesome smeared into the floor.

"Your sultan is dead," boomed the ebon colossus, flexing his hands, "and many more will be joining him before this night is through." As the words left his lips, he tensed to spring among them.

Vizek pushed his way through the mailed throng. "Unbeliever! Your death will be slow and painful."

The men hesitated, looking at each other. There was a tense silence. Then one of the guards, lowering his shield, let his sword slip to the floor. Another stepped forward and did the same, the steel ringing hollowly on the marble.

"What is the meaning of this? Your sultan lies dead!" hissed Vizek.

"He was a man accursed," said the first soldier.

"li'ana al mubarak hu shihadati!" proclaimed the second. "He cavorted with demons."

Others murmured their agreement. "And you were part of his evil," accused yet another. "Abducting citizens for that vile *thing* controlling him."

An angry buzz rippled throughout the room and soldiers gripped their weapons, staring intently at the chief treasurer as he sought to back away from them. He found his path blocked by a wall of interlocking shields. He turned in fright, his face pale as they closed in. "No! It was he that made me do it, don't you see?" His pleas went unheeded as the armoured men closed in menacingly around him. Then, as one, they seemed to crash in and Vizek was buried under a wave of slamming shields and deadly flickering blades. There was one last high-pitched scream then the shields had parted and a barely recognizable figure slipped wetly to the floor.

"So ends the lives of all traitors!" spat a soldier. The others slammed the hilts of their swords against their shields with a wild shout— "Hai!"

As the echo of that proclamation died out, Bohun stood motionless.

"Well?" he growled.

The soldiers stared back at him. Then a guard stepped forward. Retrieving his fallen sword, he rose with it in his hand. Holding it by the blade, offered the pommel to the half-naked Damzullahan. Bohun stared hard into the man's eyes. Like most soldiers of that little oasis city, these men came from a long line of desert warriors. Quick to call down vengeance on their enemies, they were quick to bond in a brotherhood of blood.

"You killed two of our men," the guard said tranquilly. "The blessed god demands that we extract vengeance for that. But it was in self-defence against the directions of a madman. By ridding us of him, you have redeemed yourself. Evil dwells in the tunnels under the palace. Many of us have lost loved ones to it. We did nothing to save them and for that we are damned. We must flee and return to burn this place to the ground. I see in your eyes that you have no such plans. Take this sword, then, and do what you will. May it serve you better than it has served me."

Bohun took the hilt and nodded grimly. The guard stepped away. His head was lowered, whether in shame or in reverence, the Damzullahan neither knew nor cared. The soldiers parted from before the door and, walking through them, Bohun stalked silently from the chamber.

A flight of stairs wound downward and, gritting his teeth, he quickened his pace, coming down them at a run.

He was inside one of the four onion domed towers of the palace. Though he did not know the layout, his sandaled feet were set on a course more resolute than if he had been guided by the brightest desert star. At last his feet hit the marbled floor and he came across an antechamber decorated with friezes and murals. A rug covered the centre of the room. Opening the door at the far end, he found himself gazing down the shadowed length of the hall where he had first been received. The highchair stood ghostly silent now. He pulled the door closed again and stepped back with a frown into the antechamber. He turned his attention to the rug and, moving over to it, flung it aside. He was not surprized to see a big brass ring set in the floor beneath. Smiling grimly, he gripped the ring with one hand and tugged. A section came up easily in his hand, revealing a set of stone steps leading into darkness. He came down that stair silently, the crescent steel clenched in his fist. This was undoubtedly the way Vizek had come when he had blown the dust into his face after he had fallen through the floor trap. Down here was where the evil lived. Thoughts of Dana and their liberty were pushed to the corners of his mind now. Here, in these tunnelled depths, was an abomination not of this earth. Every fibre of his being cried out and would not rest until it had been wiped from existence.

A torch was bracketed on the wall to his left and he took it down. To his right was the thick door with the grille through which Vizek had blown the sleep dust. To one side of it, he saw a rusted set of keys hanging from a nail on the wall. He thought of the prisoner in his cell beyond that door and took them down. Fumbling, he finally turned the right one in the lock. Coming swiftly down the small steps he moved across the corridor, waving the torch to and fro until he made out the iron bars of his cell.

"Man! Do you yet live?" he hissed out into the darkness. A stirring of chains told him all he needed to know. He padded up to the bars. "I am setting you free."

The man blinked up at him stupidly. "The sultan?"

"Dead. Are there any more down here?"

The man shuddered and huddled into himself. He shook his head. "Gone... all gone beyond the door through which you came. I heard their screams, though. The feeder... how did you survive it? Is it dead?"

Bohun was silent as he groped with the keys. Finally, he pulled the rusted door open. Unchaining the man, he lifted him to his feet. "Come," he growled, and half dragged him out into the corridor. He held the torch high in one fist, his head craning forward to scan the lapping shadows. Then they had made it up through the doorway and out onto the foot of the stair. The man squinted painfully in the glare of the light from above. Bohun gripped him hard by the shoulder and stared into his face.

"By Chaka, man, go! Go and don't look back." With that, he propelled him onto the steps. Giving him one last look, the man turned and began clambering shakily up the stair. Raising his sword, Bohun turned and loped back into the darkness. He passed the door on his right and followed the left-hand wall as it curved round to the left.

He did not have far to go. A blue light began to bathe the corridor and he felt the breath of a clammy draught on his naked limbs. At last, he came to a square cut chamber. As he neared, he slowed, looking dazedly at the sight before him. Here the blue glow was at its strongest, pulsating from a great rock that stood on a waist high pedestal in the centre of the room. From it were spun glistening silvery strands, stretching outward in all directions from floor to wall and ceiling like a monstrous web. As he gazed on it, he felt the pulsing of the blue veined stone like an insidious heartbeat. It shuddered through him, throbbed inside his skull and deep inside his own heart as if seeking to coerce every living part of him. It was as if, somehow, those vibrations could take control of his very actions. He thought of Akim Harrad and the grotesque thing that had lived within him, and shook with revulsion. Remembering the sword in his hand, he bared his teeth and stepped forward. Even as he did, he was bombarded with a powerful wave of energy that thrust knife-like into his brain.

Fool to think that the thing did not have ways of defending itself!

He staggered and would have fallen but for the determination inside him. He cried out and, though his brain felt as if it were being ripped apart, he still stood. He was frozen, unable to move or form a coherent thought. The gigantic web began to vibrate now, rippling in seductive, silvery waves. A strand parted from the ceiling and came drifting down, almost ethereal in its lightness. Delicately, it swam out, reaching sinuously toward the invader in its domain. It curled effortlessly around his shoulders, the tip wavering inquisitively before his eyes. Touching his forehead with a light caress, a thrill of static energy washed through him. It slithered round and, questing, entered his left nostril. Slowly, it began to thread its way upward. He was held in a rigid paroxysm of ecstasy, his sword hanging in one hand, the torch burning forgotten in the other. He felt something touch his thoughts and it was as if the universe opened up before his eyes.

The thing was communicating with him.

7

Words and images formed inside his mind in a language he did not know. A language that he yet, somehow, understood.

He saw a black emptiness pinpricked with tiny glittering stars. Through that emptiness came a blue-veined rock, spinning silently through the void... Impersonally, Bohun's mind's eye took in all that he saw.

Through the uncharted chasms of space and the raging infernos of the deepest nebulae it continued its eon-spanning journey. Untold millennia drifted by as, deep inside that rock, life lay dormant, awaiting the right moment to awaken.

Then came a yellow sun and a vast object that rose up in the form of a blue-green world. Through the atmosphere of that world it fell, ice and fragments burning as it screamed through the sky to land in the hot, desert night. There it lay; smouldering in a bubbling crater, as life, at last, began to stir.

The men that found the stone brought it to their city, proclaiming in triumph that the gods had blessed them. Their ruler guarded it jealously, marvelling at its radiance— an aura that was truly of the heavens. Afraid that it would become prey to thieves, he housed it in a secret chamber in the tunnels beneath his palace. At night he would come and sit before the pedestal upon which it was placed. There, gazing on it, he sought to learn wisdom from the gods. In the morning, his eyes would have a far, haunted look and he would speak strangely to his advisors. They became worried for him and sought to curb these nocturnal visits. One night, they followed him down, seeking to dissuade him from his obsession. With the dawn, the sultan alone came up from the tunnels. The advisors were never seen or heard from again.

Now the scene shifted, and he saw the chamber within which he stood. He saw the lifeforce of the strange stone grow from pale to a deep throbbing blue. He saw its tendrils spreading out before Akim Harrad as he sat in a trance-like state. He saw them reach out to the walls and the floor and the ceiling, weaving an impossible web before him. Then, finally, it whispered to him its most guarded secrets. A tendril entered, even as it had Bohun, through his nostril and began to attach itself to his mind... then, as the power grew, another and yet another tendril would come, entering through his mouth and ears. At last the star stone was strong enough. At last it had found its perfect host and could plant its alien seed. Inside something began to grow... and the thing within needed to feed.

Only one man was aware of Akim Harrad's terrible secret. That man was Vizek, who, with designs of his own, arranged for strangers and women to be snatched from the streets. There, before the pulsating blue stone from the stars, he watched as captives were fed to the unwholesome lifeform that lived within his ruler. He watched from the shadows, knowing revulsion yet also a perverse pleasure. He revelled in the screams from its victims—the young girls and women that he brought to be devoured alive.

But it was not enough.

The feeder needed to reproduce. It needed to spread out among this new world. A slave-girl was brought into the chamber. A young woman whose skin glistened like polished ebony. As she was led before the stone, the web began to vibrate and hum a strange harp-like melody. Stood before the pedestal, Akim Harrad regarded her with lust in his eyes. He lay with her then, copulating with her in the dust as cries of anguish were torn from the woman's lips... the seed had again been sown. This time in the womb.

Bohun's mind's eye viewed these scenes dispassionately. He was not aware of his own existence. But suddenly, sensation began to stir within him. He felt pain… searing, jagged pain. Slowly then with growing realization, Bohun began to waken. Sight and sound hit him simultaneously and he reeled back, eyes flying wide. The torch in his hand had burned down and was starting to scorch the flesh of his thigh. It was this pain that had brought him out of his trance. As he staggered back, the mind link was broken, and the tendril whipped out of his nostril. At that moment, Bohun looked around, seeing many tendrils weaving sinuously before him. He felt the steel in his hand and, with a wild shout, struck out, severing those that came nearest him. They parted like cobwebs before his flashing sword. The blue-veined rock on the pedestal filled his vision now. With each throbbing pulse his head pounded with pain and he struck out again, moving forward with only one thought in his mind—to destroy. He brought up the torch in his left hand and flung it at the collapsing web. There was a flare and a whoosh as it struck. Blue flame rippled as it caught in the glittering strands.

Deep inside his mind, he felt a scream of mental anguish. It came from the stone, he knew. It threatened to split open his skull, but he staggered on. Then the blue flames had raced along the collapsing web and devoured it. With supernatural quickness the rock became enveloped. That flame was cold, colder than the space between the stars, and Bohun backed away in fear. The scream grew to an unbearable pitch then suddenly the rock pitched forward. It crashed headlong to the floor, splintering into two separate halves. From it a green mist evaporated and then the scream was silenced. Impossibly, the blue fire raged on, devouring the rock and the remnants of the collapsing web. Finally, it died out altogether and all that was left were stiffened strands of web and the two frosted halves of the stone lying broken on the floor. Frost gleamed everywhere in the chamber.

Cautiously, Bohun stepped toward the pedestal, particles of ice crunching under his sandals. He stared at the sundered halves of the rock for an instant then brought his sword down—once, twice, in quick succession. They shivered to bits under the fury of his strokes and those pieces he ground to dust beneath his heel. Shivering, he stepped back out of the chamber.

He stood as if in a daze, trying to comprehend all that had happened. Then he lifted his head as fear clutched his heart anew.

Dana!

He wheeled and raced back down the corridor. He barely saw the stairs that he bounded up to emerge out into the antechamber. His thoughts were a riot of confusion and fear. Images and words came back to him in disjointed flashes. He remembered the visions in his head... the thing's need to reproduce... Akim Harrad copulating with his wife before the blue stone. Then he remembered his wife's words to him in the sultan's throne room— *"Evil walks here. I have stared into the dark heart of Chaka. It is too late for me... too late..."*

The memory of those words hit him with the impact of a thunderbolt. He came out of the antechamber, pelting full tilt down the length of the hall. He had no idea where he was going, only a blind sense of reasoning to trace steps where he had already been. He was dimly aware of people shouting in panic, fleeing like shadows through the archways of the palace as they sought to escape. A mailed soldier passed him, giving him a wide berth, seeing the crazed look in his eyes. Then he had ploughed headlong into a slim white shape. He reached out, gripping a pale arm in his hand. He swung the woman round and the bangles on her limbs clashed startlingly. She fell to her knees, painted eyes wide with fright.

"Dana! Where is she?" he snarled. The girl looked up dazedly. He shook her roughly. "Where?"

She cried out and looked back quickly over her shoulder. "In the harem, she—please... let me go!" She twisted in his grasp and he released her. She sped away but he was already moving, coming to the red silk hanging at the far end of the hall. He ripped the gauze aside with one hand and flung it to the floor. He came down a carpeted hallway, emerging out into a spacious marble chamber. In contrast to the rest of the palace, all here was still and calm.

A single copper oil lamp burned from its bracket on the wall. Cushions and rugs were strewn on the floor between couches strategically positioned for the art of seduction. Beyond them were hangings of red and yellow gauze. He moved in silently and, as he did, he saw the shadowed outline of a woman lying on a couch behind a silk curtain. His heart in his mouth, he approached slowly and, with one hand, reached up and thrust the hanging aside.

Bathed in the light of the glow from the single lamp, Dana lay, her sleek ebon skin slick with sweat, her breast rising and falling in slow rhythm. She lay naked on a divan strewn with leopard skins. Her eyelids fluttered now, and her head turned slightly as Bohun knelt down beside her. One hand reached out and a smile curved her lips. The slender arm seemed to lose its strength and then collapse, her fingers tracing a soft caress down his chiselled face. At the side of the divan lay an overturned goblet, its fragrant nectar forming a small puddle on the floor.

"Poison," he breathed. Gripping her hand, he pressed it to his lips and squeezed his eyes shut.

"Dana..." The word came as a tortured gasp.

"I could not live with it inside me, Bohun," she rasped. "It is the only way. Mourn for me and weep, my love. But then live. Do not bury me in the dust of this land. Bury me deep in the earth by the water and sing the songs of my ancestors. In T'agulla's domain I will await you. He will guard and keep my spirit... safe..." Her breath ended in a sigh and she stiffened. A trickle of blood crept from her mouth and she was dead.

8

Fishermen along the banks of the river Zallam paused from the casting of their nets to witness the strange sight that greeted them in the early light of dawn. Mist crawled along the reeds and drifted out over the river as the sun began to break against the sky. A raft came moving almost solemnly down the waters, poled by a well-built white skinned youth with close cropped hair. At his side were two people. One was an olive-skinned woman wrapped in a long grey cloak against the dawn's chill. The other was a tall, large black man. It was the latter that aroused the fishermen's curiosity most. He was wide shouldered, wearing the robes and headdress of a desert tribesman. His face was chiselled as if from iron and he stared grimly ahead, looking to neither left nor right. His dark eyes were hard as flint. Belted at his waist was a curved scimitar in a metal worked scabbard and at his feet lay a long object wrapped in a linen shroud. He stood brace legged over this object and the lithe men along the riverbank knew him for a man in mourning. Then the mists had curled over them and they were gone, leaving the fishermen to draw up their nets and wonder if they had ever really seen them at all.

That afternoon the raft came to a fertile pasture and the well-built youth led his companions through long grasses to a glade between bowed trees. There a grave was dug and the man, who had once been the champion of Damzullah, laid his wife to rest. He sung the dirge of his people and the songs of her ancestors. The sky was dark and the sun an extinguishing red flame when all was done.

A day later they arrived at a small trading outpost. Tents flapped drearily in the wind and dark eyed men squatted in the sand, eyeing the strangers suspiciously, their hands never far from their knives. Dogs yapped in the heat and the stench of camels was unbearable. A caravan master, ready to leave for the coast, offered the warrior from Damzullah a job as guardsman. One of their number had gone down with desert fever and could no longer continue the journey. Farewells between the three travellers were brief.

"Where will you go, Tyrun?" asked Bohun. He looked past him to his wife standing with head bowed.

"Anya has relatives in a township to the east. We will go there. Who knows, maybe one day I will take up my sword and follow you into paths of glory," he grinned.

The giant black nodded and slapped a hand on his shoulder. "Look after your wife and child. Fish, hunt and know the company of good men."

Tyrun nodded. "And you?"

Bohun shrugged. "Wherever the gods will me they will find my sword arm ready."

*

In the long weeks that followed, turmoil swept over the city state of Ibn-Shahk. The palace was burned to the ground by its citizens. Those faithful to her dead ruler, Akim

Harrad, were seized and stoned to death.

Eventually, soldiers were sent from the outlying provinces to deal with the unrest. They came marching up through the gates to find a city deep in the throes of violence. Order had broken down as rival gangs fought openly in the streets. Bitter enmities flared up and the little oasis city found itself a battleground for a short but fierce civil war. At the end of it, Ibn-Shahk was a smoking wasteland, its citizens scattered. Merchants that fled told stories of a gigantic black warrior who had brought doom upon the city, slaying its sultan. One man, who claimed to have been held prisoner beneath the crypts of the palace, told another tale. He told of a despot ruler who preyed upon his own people and who worshipped strange and terrible gods. He spoke of a swordsman from the hot savannahs of the south who helped rid the land of its curse. Though a search was made along the outlying provinces, no evidence of this man was ever found, and the story passed into folklore.

*

The noise and dust of the small coastal outpost stifled in the afternoon heat. No breeze blew in from the ocean and the sea was like a mirror lying flat under the blazing sun.

Bohun stared out from the shack that served as a tavern at the great warships lying offshore. Everywhere armoured men moved, their breast plates flashing like burnished gold.

"Out of the way!" roared a big soldier, barging up and brushing aside scrawny natives that held out their begging bowls to him. He kicked them into the dust and, swaggering into the tavern, doffed his crested helmet. Sweeping back his red cloak, he crashed into a rickety chair and rested his iron grieved boots up on the table. "Wine, damn you!" he shouted at a native woman who scurried away to do his bidding. He swivelled his head, seeing Bohun leaning against the open window, regarding him.

"Ho, a big lad, this one! You're not from these parts. Whence you hail?"

"Damzullah."

"Never heard of it. Shit hole, is it? That why you left?" He laughed uproariously at his own jest, drawing appreciative titters from the other soldiers sat either gambling or drinking in the cool shaded den.

Pushing his way out from the window frame, Bohun kicked up a stool and sat opposite him. He jerked his head. "That fleet. Where is it headed?"

The big soldier blinked at him, noticing the easy grace with which he moved, the hilt of the big curved scimitar at his side. "Where have you been? There's a war on, lad. We're the royal fleet of Valentia. Sent out by the emperor's decree. We're on our way to Dionyssa to crush the oily bastards and send their fleet to hades."

"I would join you."

The big soldier made to laugh then stopped, running a hand over his jaw and reaching for the cask the serving girl had just placed on the table. He took a swig and wiped a bronze wrist guard over his lips. "Well, it's true we are short of men. I can't promise a standard uniform, not until we reach Dionyssa, but if you can keep a steady pace with an oar—well, we'll need you. That sword will have to go though." He pointed at the two-handed hilt jutting from Bohun's waist. "Only standard issue spatha for infantry, whether you're a general or recruit." He slapped a hand on the metal scabbard at his own side.

Bohun nodded. The big soldier laughed and, thumping his fist down on the roughhewn boards, pushed the wine cask over to him. "Then welcome to the army, lad! Onward to Dionyssa!"

Swinging up the wine cask, the Damzullahan gave a mocking salute before taking a long swig and slamming it back down on the table again.

"On to Dionyssa," he said.

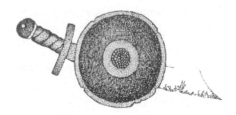

TROLLS ARE DIFFERENT
Susan Murrie Macdonald

The songbirds sang as I approached the swamp. A cool breeze blew from the east. I didn't see or hear anything beyond the birds singing and the leaves blowing in the breeze, but I knew I was being watched.

The trolls don't let anyone approach the swamp unobserved.

I set down the basket I was carrying and waited. Despite the lightening charm on the basket, I was glad to put it down; my hands were getting tired. I didn't have to wait long before I heard footsteps splashing in the water. A minute later, I smiled when I saw the troll shaman, Chirbatti. I stuck out my tongue at her.

Chirbatti returned the gesture. "'Lo, Mar."

My name is Marana, but her tusks made human speech difficult and like most trolls she shortens words whenever possible.

Humans clasp hands or hold up empty palms when greeting people to show they're unarmed. Trolls look at things differently than humans. To a troll only a fool would admit to being unarmed. So they stick out their tongues, like snakes, to taste what the air tells of the person greeting them. Trolls consider that far more sensible.

Chirbatti's face was almost human, other than the boar-like tusks, bear-like black nose, and cat-like yellow eyes, she wore a wicker wreath over her braided black and green hair. An ordinary human might laugh at her wreath: it looked like she had a failed attempt at a basket on her head. A troll would respect it as the symbol of her rank and position. Personally, I thought it looked ridiculous, especially with her horns protruding from beneath the wreath, but I was polite enough to keep my opinion to myself. Her horns were rather like a goat's, but polished and painted green, the way city women paint their fingernails.

On the other hand, I'm not a beauty myself: short, chubby, with hair going from copper to white. I was no flower when I was a girl, so it's no surprise now that I'm near to a half century that my visage does not make men swoon.

"What you got, Mar? Good bribe?" Chirbatti asked hopefully.

"Five pounds of rice, the first of the harvest. And three blackberry tarts with a stay-fresh charm as a bribe," I replied. Not that my tarts need a stay-fresh charm. They'll be eaten before they have a chance to spoil.

Trading with trolls, it's traditional for the one initiating the exchange to offer a lagniappe to show how much they want to make the trade. Between old friends like Chirbatti and me, a token bribe like home-baked tarts is acceptable, but if I hadn't included something extra, Chirbatti would've thought I wasn't interested in the trade… despite the fact that my village and her clan have been trading partners for generations. I've known Chirbatti all my life, and I'm still not sure whether she actually thinks it's a bribe or whether it's just a translation error because our language is hard for her.

"What you want?" Chirbatti asked.

"Smoked fish. Pound for pound."

Chirbatti nodded. Trolls, thank goodness, don't believe in making bartering a long-drawn out process. Not like the city-folk to the north, who'll take half an hour to sell you a bushel of fruit.

"I have more rice," I mentioned casually, as if Chirbatti didn't know that rice paddies produce more than one basketful of rice.

"Might have more fish," she allowed.

"Maybe you have some sausage?"

Swamp trolls make excellent sausage… as long as you just chew and swallow and don't think about what they make sausages from.

As we were negotiating amounts, Chirbatti tilted her head at an angle.

"What do you hear?" I asked. Trolls' ears are different from humans'. Their ears are bigger than ours, and they hear farther, but they hear low sounds better than high sounds. Chirbatti can't enjoy the songs of the flutter-flowers or the orioles; she can barely hear them.

"Horse."

That surprised me. I don't think anyone within twenty miles owns a horse. We use oxen to plough, and when we travel, we go on our own two feet.

A tired horse trotted up the road, a half unconscious soldier slumped in the saddle. I clicked at it and made the nonsense noises one does with a strange animal. "Easy there." I patted its neck. "Easy. Good boy. Rest now."

Chirbatti and I untangled the rider from the saddle and harness and helped him down. Chirbatti had a waterskin and poured some water over his dusty face and into his mouth.

Beneath the dust and bruises, the rider was pale. Too pale.

"Lost blood," Chirbatti observed. I nodded; she was right.

"Harv- Harvans coming," he sputtered once he was able to speak. "Call up the militia to delay them and send word to the fort at Sallum."

I frowned. Our village has no militia. Those few of us with any fighting ability or pretence to being warriors had been conscripted to fight the Harvans. Sallum was a three-four-day journey on foot. The horse was too exhausted to attempt it, even if any messenger I sent could stay on its back for more than an hour without falling off.

"Let's take him to your lodge so we can tend him properly," I suggested

"Why not your cottage? Him human. Tend in human home."

"Your place is closer. Besides, there's white fever in the village."

"Might be frightened if he wake in a troll lodge," she said.

I fingered the tattered remnants of his uniform. "The king's soldiers are supposed to be brave."

I had to cast a lightening charm before we could get him back on the horse. The beast whinnied and nickered nervously as we led it into the swamp.

"You, your people, hide in swamp 'til soldiers go," Chirbatti suggested.

Taking refuge in the swamp and waiting out the Harvans was probably the most sensible plan, but I knew some of the villagers would refuse. Despite having lived next to the swamp and the trolls all their lives, too many of my people were uncomfortable with both. That's why I'm the main contact between our people and the trolls. For generations beyond counting, the village witch has been the liaison with the troll shaman.

"We might," I allowed, "but some will fear their crops will be destroyed and their chickens and goats stolen if they're not there to guard them."

"Better dead crops than dead people," Chirbatti pointed out. "Soldiers prob'ly steal an'mals anyway, then kill them."

"There is wisdom in your words."

"I wise," Chirbatti agreed.

The horse didn't like the wet footing of the swamp, but we led it to Chirbatti's lodge so we could tend its rider. Her lodge looked like a giant beaver dam, half wood, half wicker. Inside there were four empty hammocks. We stripped the soldier naked and laid him in Chirbatti's son's hammock. Then we washed his wounds, first with clean water, then with wine. I raided Chirbatti's herb supply to make a poultice. I am an herbwife as well as a hearthwitch.

He stirred as we tended his wounds. "Get word to the fort at Sallum."

"Whom should we tell them brought the message? What is your name?"

"Corporal Delus." His eyes opened, he saw Chirbatti, and he fainted.

That's not fair. He may not have fainted at the sight of her. Soiled rushes covered the floor. Maybe the smell of them got to him. They were overdue for changing.

Spare clothes hung from pegs on the wall. Sausages and a ham – probably an alligator-ham – hung from the ceiling. Most troll lodges are only one room. Beyond the oilcloth curtain that served as a door, Chirbatti had a second room, a shrine for her shamanic duties.

"You have paper?" I asked.

Chirbatti grunted an affirmative and fetched paper and ink and two lizard-talon quills. I wrote a message carefully, then rewrote it on a second piece of paper.

"What wrong with that one?" Chirbatti asked.

"If I send two messengers north, there's a better chance of the message getting through."

Chirbatti grunted her approval and began writing two messages herself.

"Pity you witch, Mar."

I nodded. If I were a sorceress or a wizard, I could send a message magically, but I'm only a hearthwitch and a herbwife. I could no more speak with someone a hundred miles away than I could fly.

"You're a shaman," I reminded her.

"Can tell ancestors, ask pass word shaman other clans, but," she shrugged, "ancestors not listen much, not co'p'rate."

I nodded. Trolls look at things differently than humans, and dead trolls have a different perspective than live trolls.

*

I made sure Delus was as comfortable as possible under the circumstances, then led his horse back to the village. "Ronek, I need a favour," I told my grandnephew.

"Yes, Aunt Marana?"

"Find Brevara and Tonek. Bring them here. Then tell everyone, yes, I mean *every one*, to meet me at the grange hall as quickly as possible. Brevara and Tonek first, though."

"Yes, Auntie."

I set about brewing some potions and medicines. Brevara showed up before I had finished. "Have some bread and tea, lass," I invited. It's best to feed people before asking them for favours.

"Do you think you could walk to Sallum without getting killed?"

"Like as not," she agreed.

The young are overconfident.

"I need a message delivered to the fort at Sallum."

"Could I ride that horse you have tied up behind your cottage?"

"Only if you want to take twice as long. That poor beast is exhausted. It needs rest and gentle care. I wouldn't count on it to go a furlong without floundering."

"Oh." Her face fell.

"A wounded soldier collapsed just outside the village. He had a message that *must* get through. The Harvan army is coming. We need to get word to the soldiers at Sallum and convince them to come here. Not sure which will be harder, you making it to Sallum in one piece or convincing them to come here. Be persuasive."

She tucked the message into her bodice. I frowned. As if that weren't the first place a bandit or soldier searching her would check.

*

It took a while to gather the villagers together. Plough-men can leave their crops unattended for a little while, and the soil won't mind waiting. If you're in the middle of baking a loaf of bread, or changing a baby's dirty loincloth, you can't drop everything and come running. Or if the smith is forging a new plough, he must strike while the iron is hot, or the plough will be ruined and break in the field.

"Listen carefully," I said. "Trouble is coming." I waited to make sure I had their attention, then continued, "The Harvan army is on its way here."

Then I waited again for them to calm down. When I got tired of them chittering like squirrels and shrieking like crows, I took a wooden whistle out of my pocket and blew it as loudly as I could.

"Chirbatti and I have already sent for help." I took a deep breath, waiting for that to sink in. "We have sent for help, but it will take a week, maybe longer, for help to arrive. The Harvan army will be here in a day or two."

"What good will help do us in a week or more?" the blacksmith yelled.

"We can't fight them; they'd squash us like ants," I acknowledged. "We have to outwit them, stall them so that help has time to arrive. We will pretend to welcome them, pretend that we're glad to have them come 'rescue' us from the northern tyrant."

"Not hard to pretend," the miller yelled out.

Others laughed, and agreed under their breaths.

I've heard there are lands where the king is adored, but I've never travelled far enough to find such a place.

"If we try to fight them and don't kill *all* of them, they will demolish us. So no one tries anything stupid and heroic. Let Chirbatti and me handle it," I told them.

The villagers nodded and mumbled in agreement. Amazing how telling most people 'let someone else handle it' works so well.

"You know what city-folk are like. Harvan city-folk or our own cities, they're the same. They think we're stupid, with no more brains than our oxen. So let them see what they expect to see, just ignorant peasants who couldn't possibly outwit clever soldiers in their bright, shiny armour."

Half the villagers laughed.

"We may take a few bruises, we'll certainly lose some of our supplies, but Chirbatti and I have a plan to make sure everyone survives."

SWORDS & SORCERIES

*

Chirbatti and I traced lines in the dirt from the river to the only suitable campsite along the trade-road, chanting, praying, and spellcasting as we dug our sticks in the dirt. As above, so below, as within, so without. A good spell is like cookie dough; it needs to sit and chill before it can be worked. It took us a few hours, but good spellwork can't be rushed. As we laid out the patterns, we whispered to the river, telling it to wait, but that when the time came it would be invited to follow and fill these shadows of canals. Invited and welcomed.

*

When the Harvan troops came marching in the next day, I was there waiting, waving a white shawl tied to a stick.

"I would speak with your commander."

"Out of the way, woman," one of the soldiers ordered.

I stood firm. "I must speak with your commander."

A man in a resplendent scarlet uniform slowly rode up to me. He looked like a warlord out of a ballad, ruggedly handsome, strong. About ten years my junior, I guessed. His cloak was red velvet on the outside, and what I could see of the inside looked like bear fur. He wore a golden cuirass, or at least golden-coloured. Real gold would have been too soft and too heavy. Dust from the road covered his boots, but I knew good leather when I saw it, and I suspected he could have bought half our village for the price of those boots. Two or three officers followed him.

"Who are you?" the warlord demanded.

"Marana, headwoman of this village. I've come to negotiate with you." I tried not to react when I saw the brooch on his cloak. Beautiful enamel work, although it was the pattern that caught my eye rather than the aesthetics. Intricate knotwork surrounded the royal crest of Harva, indicating he was connected to the royal family by marriage or blood, or possibly a very trusted retainer. Such a man would be dangerous. I forced myself to stay calm and my face placid.

One of his officers laughed.

"I'm listening," the commander said.

"We have no animosity against you, and I want to keep it that way." I frowned. I hadn't meant to use a big word. It would be easier to be underestimated if they thought me an ignorant peasant. "I don't want my maidens raped, nor the village lads. I don't want your troops eating a month's worth of food in one day, then trampling our fields so we can't grow more."

"Who are you to tell us what to do?" asked the officer who'd laughed at me.

"Marana, headwoman of this village," I repeated. "Do you have a priest or wizard who can determine if I speak truly? Perhaps he can also cast a spell to clear the wax from your ears."

A scrawny man riding a dapple-grey gelding came forward. He wore an elaborately embroidered cloak rather than a uniform. I recognized some of the embroidery as magic glyphs.

I bowed my head respectfully to him. "Hear my words. Judge their truth."

He made a series of elaborate hand gestures, the sort of sleight of hand stage "magicians" use to impress their audiences and muttered some words of power under his breath. Although I was only a hearthwitch rather than a sorceress, I could feel the power as he spoke his incantation.

Once he had set his spell, I spoke. "We pledge not to poison your water, steal your horses, or send guides to lead you through quicksand. In return, you agree not to ravage our village or molest our people."

"Why?" the Harvan commander asked.

"Don't you soldiers say the enemy of my enemy is my friend? We've little loyalty and less love for the king in the north. The northerners treat us like pigs. They conscript our young men and women to fight you. They're all to the east," I pointed, "that's where they think you are, instead of home tending the fields and beasts. They tax us until we can barely survive but ignore us the rest of the time. They won't lift a finger to protect us from the swamp trolls."

A scrawny fellow in fine robes fingered an amulet, then nodded to the commander. "She speaks the truth."

"And you think we are your saviours?" the commander asked.

"If you win, you probably won't be any better, but," I shrugged, "I doubt you'll be any worse."

The warlord laughed. "Very well, Marana. You have a bargain. For the next half hour. We ride on once we've watered the horses."

"No, lord, rest your horses. Rest your soldiers. They think you far from here." I pointed east again. "Your troops are surely tired of field rations. I won't stand still whilst all our supplies are stolen, but sharing with guests, well, that's a jug of milk from a different goat. We can share fresh-baked bread and good smoked sausages and new-brewed beer."

I bit back a smile, for I could see how the soldiers close enough to overhear us reacted to the word 'beer.'

*

Two or three of the older village women came and offered to wash the soldiers' clothes and blankets for a few coppers. There was some haggling, and they let themselves be argued down in price, to let the soldiers think they'd won. I wouldn't have cared if we'd washed their clothes for free, except that might have made them suspicious. All I cared about was making sure there was enough poison ivy in the water.

*

That evening, a dozen villagers brought beer for them to drink, every loaf of fresh-baked bread in the village, and troll-made sausages for their cooks to add to their stew pots

When they were halfway done eating, I signalled two of the village maidens who had come to help serve the meal and flirt with the soldiers.

"I'm surprised to see you enjoy it so," Elessa said. "I would not have expected you to enjoy such humble fare as we peasants eat."

I bit my lip, trying not to frown as she laid it on with a butter knife.

Gicara nodded. "Outlanders don't usually enjoy frog and lizard sausage."

Some of the soldiers turned green. Some dumped their bowls on the ground. One or two of the younger ones threw up. The older soldiers shrugged and kept eating.

I smiled.

"Is the beer safe?" asked one of the soldiers who had dumped his stew bowl on the ground.

I glanced at the oak keg, dipped a mug in, and took a sip. "Tastes fine to me."

The beer in the oak kegs was perfectly fine. 'Twas the

beer in the cypress kegs that I'd added a few extra herbs to. One keg in three was cypress, so our people would know not to drink from those ones.

The soldiers who drank from the cypress kegs tramped back and forth to the latrines all night, back and forth, back and forth. If I do say so myself, I brew an effective laxative.

The sun had just finished setting when the drums started. Then the whistles and rattles. And then the 'singing.'

"What's that?" one of the soldiers demanded.

I feigned a worried expression on my face. "Troll music."

Gicara looked scared. "That's troll war music," she lied. "They play that to build up their courage before they attack."

The music coming from the swamps became louder. Hollow log drums, lizard-bone whistles, cane pipes, turtle shell rattles, and the cacophonous lyrics of a troll love song. I didn't dare risk any mendacity, not knowing how strong the Harvan sorcerer's truth-spell was, so Gicara had been delegated to fib for me.

We headed back to the village, telling the soldiers how glad we were that their camp and their swords were between us and the trolls. I had arranged with Chirbatti for the concert to continue for hours.

We hoped that the troll music would make it hard for the soldiers to sleep. Tired men are cranky, and cranky men make mistakes. Except for the sentries, of course. I felt sorry for the sentries, marching all day, so I kindly cast a soporific spell on them so they could get some rest.

*

The next morning, I got up early so I could watch when the Harvan soldiers awoke. They were tired and grumpy, and about half of them were damp. Chirbatti and I had combined our spells well: the camp was flooded. Water and mud were everywhere. Sergeants were yelling at sentries for sleeping on duty.

The campfires sputtered and wouldn't stay lit, making it impossible for them to heat their porridge. The soldiers complained about wet wood. As a hearthwitch, I usually keep fires from setting chimneys ablaze. Making their fires sputter and go out was a minor adjustment to a spell I cast on a monthly basis, made easier by the fact that most of the wood was wet from Chirbatti and I having 'invited' the river to come.

*

By noon, a third of the Harvans had low fevers. Their healers demanded my entire supply of willowbark tea. I gave them half. I mercifully sent along a jar of honey to kill the taste. Willowbark tea is a good painkiller and fever-reducer, but most people say the flavour is reminiscent of ox-piss. I don't know who made the comparison. I'm not that brave myself.

In two days some of the soldiers were showing signs of white fever: dried skin like dandruff all over their faces and arms, fever, muscle weakness, lack of appetite. I told the Harvan healers it looked like white fever to me, but they scoffed. I'm just a village herbwife; what do I know? White fever is a children's disease, so perhaps army healers don't have much experience with it. Maybe once the soldiers start scratching themselves bloody they'll believe me.

There's nothing you can do about white fever but wait it out and treat the symptoms. Like most childhood diseases, it's harder on adults than it is on children. Men who catch white fever as an adult can't father children, but that's all right. There are enough Harvans in the world already.

By the fifth day, half the Harvans couldn't get out of their bedrolls in the morning. A quarter of them were sick, and another quarter were exhausted from playing nursemaid. I don't think more than five men were fit to fight. Chirbatti suggested slitting the throats of the few healthy ones. Trolls aren't immoral, they just look at things differently than humans do.

I wondered if Brevara and Tonek had made it to Sallum yet. Even if they had, the fort commander might not listen to them or believe them. If he did, troops don't march on a minute's notice. It takes time to organize supplies and issue marching orders. Since it would be infantry, not cavalry, the king's soldiers couldn't reach us any sooner than Brevara and Tonek had reached them.

I went to Chirbatti's lodge to tend Delus. Chirbatti and I worried. We were running out of delaying tactics. I had no more tricks up my sleeve.

*

"Marana, I wanted to thank you for your hospitality. My healers tell me you gave them medicines to treat our ill," the Harvan commander told me.

"Don't know I'd call it giving when they had swords at the ready," I muttered just loud enough to be heard.

He reached into his coinpurse and pulled out three silver Harvan eagles. He tossed them down to me.

"Thank you, lord." I tried to keep the note of surprise out of my voice. I failed.

"My troops and I are moving on. The river-damp doesn't agree with us."

"Safe journeys, lord." Once he was out of my village, he was no longer my headache, so I had no problem in well-wishing him. I'm only a hearthwitch. My wishes have no power.

He issued orders. His men obeyed. I wish my children had been half that obedient in their younger days. They packed up the camp and cleaned the area before marching north.

They were scarcely out of sight when Chirbatti came running. "Soldiers come," she announced.

"No, soldiers go." We both pointed north. We heard the rumbling of scores of booted feet marching, and the beating of drums. We could see clouds of dust over the road.

"I hope a small delay is better than nothing. We saved our own folk, at least."

"We save kingdom," Chirbatti insisted. "King's soldiers coming."

"There's not time for them to be on their way here yet," I told her. "There's barely time for Brevara and Tonek to have reached Sallum yet. The fort commander won't have sent any men yet."

"I tell your little human ears, I heard soldiers coming," Chirbatti insisted.

It was impossible, but she was right. We soon heard the thwack of bowstrings and the whistling of arrows as the king's troops fell upon the Harvan soldiers. Then we heard metal clanging against metal as both sides drew swords.

The smell was like hog-butchering time. The cold tang of spilt blood, and other, worse odours as dying men emptied both bowels and bladders.

More men than I'd ever seen in one place in my life, all of them in the blue tunic and trews of the king's army.

After a bit, an officer in a fur-trimmed cape came riding

up on a big black stallion. "You, there! I seek the Lady Cherbadda. Where might I find her?"

Chirbatti grinned.

"This is the Shaman Chirbatti, she who speaks for the swamp trolls. Is that whom you mean?" I pointed to her.

"Cherbadda, Chirbatti, close enough. The king himself bid me give you this." He pulled a gold bracelet off his wrist and handed it down to her. "The king's wizard received a message from the shaman of the forest trolls, that the Harvans were invading, and that it was thanks to you we had warning."

"Ancestors came through." Chirbatti whistled in excitement. "Must burn sage tonight to thank them. Ancestors usually unreliable."

We were both pleased, but surprised. She put the bracelet on her arm. Trolls are like magpies: they have a weakness for shiny things.

The ruckus was beginning to die down, so she and I trudged to the battlefield to tend the wounded. Our soldiers set up camp where the Harvans had been.

An hour later, two soldiers came up to me. "Are you Headwoman Marana?"

"I am. Are you wounded?"

"You're under arrest for treason," the younger of the two said as the older one grabbed my arms and pulled them behind my back.

"Arrest for treason? What madness is this?" I asked as I kicked first his ankle and then his shin.

He swore but didn't let go of me. The younger one pulled a length of leather cord out of his beltpouch and began tying my hands behind me.

They dragged me, kicking and screaming, to their commander.

"The traitress, Marana," they introduced me as they thrust me on the muddy ground before his feet.

"You are under arrest for giving aid and comfort to the enemy," the commander informed me.

"I did no such thing. It was a ruse. I had to stall them until our messengers could reach you."

"The message was sent by troll-magic, days ago."

"'Troll-magic' is different from human wizardry. Neither Chirbatti nor I were confident the message would get through, so we sent messengers to make sure the fort at Sallum was notified."

"Your people tell me you are a minor hearthwitch. Obviously you are jealous of the mighty troll sorceress," he accused.

I tried not to laugh in his face. Chirbatti couldn't light a candle with magic.

"We weren't sure she could relay the message through the spirits, so we sent mortal messengers as a failsafe. All that I did to the Harvans, was to delay them until you could arrive," I explained.

I struggled with the cord binding my wrists and cast a spell to loosen it. I had it nearly undone when the soldiers grabbed me and dragged me to my feet.

I broke away and ran as fast as I could.

I was forced to take refuge in the swamp. Northerners ignore us except at tax time, so I should be able to come out of hiding soon. And in the meantime, Chirbatti's a good cook. I just wish she didn't snore so much.

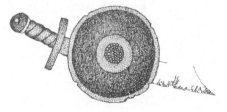

CHAIN OF COMMAND
Geoff Hart

The towering woman placed a proportionally large hand on the sarcophagus. "I'll remove the lid; you watch my back."

The diminutive woman nodded. "Agreed. But watch yourself too. Wouldn't surprise me a bit if it's cursed." Mouse was no primitive, her barbarian heritage notwithstanding, yet she'd been raised on supernatural tales and hadn't freed herself completely from their grip.

Freya bent her knees, grunted, and applied pressure, muscles swelling on her arms and thighs. The thick stone hesitated a moment, then lifted an inch. She took a deep breath, braced herself again, and reapplied her strength. This time, the lid slid free, falling to the floor with a crash that raised billows of ancient dust.

A dark cloud rose from the sarcophagus, towering over her despite her near seven feet of height. The cloud slowly took shape, becoming a once-muscular old man wearing a crown.

"Who dares disturb my rest?" The voice was dry, with an antique accent.

Freya stepped back to stand beside Mouse, who'd drawn her sword. "I believe it's these two gentlemen you wish to speak with." She swept her free hand back towards the two sorcerers who'd led them here; her own sword had found its way into her hand.

The fat mage glanced at the thin mage, who tittered nervously. The former nodded his chin towards the spectre, and the thin one stepped forward. As he did, he raised his hands before his face and began to weave a complex pattern, hands leaving a faintly glowing trail. The spectre snorted and raised its own hands, weaving a different pattern bright enough to leave afterimages on the eyes. The thin mage finished his pattern, and smiled a thin smile at the spectre. Neither the smile nor the glowing image before him had the slightest effect on the lash of dark flame that shot from the spectre's hands, curled lasciviously around the mage, and — before he could draw breath to scream — left him a smoking cinder that slowly collapsed under its own weight, like untended ash falling from a well-used cigar.

"Oh dear," said the fat one, and pissed himself.

*

Several days earlier, the king's advisor had frowned down at the two women from his throne-like chair, atop a raised platform. "My agents tell me you're both skilled with a sword. This barbarian," he nodded at the 7-foot woman who was clad, incongruously, in a well-tailored pair of breeches and billowing silk shirt, accessorized by a sword nearly as long as her companion was tall slung over her shoulder. "*Her*, I have confidence in. She has the look of a hardened killer."

The "hardened killer" grinned. The smaller woman glanced to her side, craning her neck to take in the full scope of her companion. At first glance, the giant seemed little different from the many large men and women she'd humbled when they underestimated her. She'd grown up in a barbarian village, where such giants were the norm, even among the women.

"But you?" He looked at the smaller woman and snorted.

"You have, I grant you, a certain litheness of motion, but a tender urbanite such as yourself? I should think it would serve you poorly against this one."

"I might surprise you. And her."

"You might, and you might speculate that I don a woman's garb each night when I return home. *Proof* is what I need. If you're to surprise me in any kind of pleasant way, now would be a good time. One or two passes at each other with your swords, if you please. I'm keen to see with my own eyes how you both move."

The taller woman looked down at the short one. "Freya. Are you willing?"

The other returned her gaze with equanimity. "Mouse." Her eyes narrowed dangerously as the tall one's grin widened. "Aye, I'm willing—but only to first blood. I wouldn't rob our King of your evidently remarkable skills should I chance to win."

"And should you, by chance, lose—which you will?"

Mouse's fierce answering grin reflected Freya's. "Well, then, neither would I wish to deprive our king of myself, so best if it were only first blood. Not *last*, if you take my meaning."

Freya found herself liking the small woman, and swept a deep bow. "On guard, then."

Mouse curtsied without ever taking her eyes from the other woman, but misliked how easily the big woman drew her sword over her shoulder. The ease of drawing such a long sword did not, itself, alarm her; she was amply familiar with large, powerful men, and not a few large, powerful women. It was how she held the blade one-handed that concerned her, not to mention the efficiency of the motion— the lack of swagger was a particular concern. Men seemed insecure over whether size alone was sufficient to intimidate, and felt a need to elaborate. Most never quite mastered the use of their size.

For her part, Freya watched the smaller women with a keen eye. Big men were easily handled, as they relied too much on their strength, but this small woman moved far too fluidly for her liking, and the sabre she drew from her scabbard, an inch-wide length of polished, well-maintained steel, drew the eye. This was not a lady's weapon, worn for show; it was a fighting sword, and well used from the look of it.

"Milady Mouse", she bowed, never taking her eyes off her foe.

"Milady Freya," the other woman replied, watching every bit as warily.

With that, the two stepped apart, raised their blades to salute, then approached each other. Freya was content to keep her opponent at the comfortable distance permitted by her sword's greater length; Mouse, for her part, knew she'd need to come within reach of that blade long enough to lunge and draw blood. In a real fight, she might have been tempted to let the larger woman tire herself from swinging that intimidating weight of steel, while judiciously arranging to remain beyond its reach. Here, it seemed wiser to rely on speed. Feinting high, she stutter-stepped close enough to tempt Freya's swing. Had Mouse been even a hand taller, that swing might have cost her a lock of hair, and possibly some scalp; as it was, the bigger woman misjudged Mouse's speed. Mouse ducked nimbly beneath the swing and tapped Freya's thigh and forearm an eyeblink before the return stroke of that enormous blade caught her across the back and propelled her, staggering, across the floor. The two women sprang backwards, disengaging, eyes narrowed.

"Enough!" called the king's advisor.

"But neither of us has drawn blood," Mouse observed.

"And neither shall you. You're no good to me if you kill each other."

"Agreed," boomed the taller one. Freya's voice was uncommonly deep for a woman, though not out of proportion to the depth and breadth of her chest.

"For now," whispered the shorter one, drawing an amused glance from Freya.

The advisor cleared his throat. "You've been chosen to protect two seekers in my service." He pulled a cord that dangled beside his seat, and a bell tinkled. Two men entered the room clad in robes; the first was fat enough to be nearly round, and his robes were a simple midnight blue; the other was thin as a glaive, with an equally hooked nose, and his wine-red robe was cluttered with a mass of obscure symbols, picked out in gold embroidery.

"Seekers?"

The two women had spoken simultaneously; they met each other's eyes, and shared a grin.

"This one's Thomas. He'll be subordinate, but you'll follow any instructions he provides." The thin one waved a hand coyly at Mouse, blushing, and tried to meet her eyes. She snorted and returned her gaze to the advisor.

"And this is Mathias. He will command your expedition, and you'll follow his command, as does Thomas." The round one gazed ostentatiously at the ceiling, as if watching things only he could see. Mouse found herself wanting to poke him to capture his attention. Instead, she sheathed her sword before she could give in to temptation.

The two women exchanged gazes. Mouse nodded. "And what might they seek," wondered Freya aloud.

"Why the truth, of course." The advisor evaded their

eyes. The two women exchanged glances.

This time, Mouse spoke. "*Whose* truth?"

The king's advisor frowned. "We chose you for your wit, small one, as we chose your companion for her brawn. Please don't convince us we chose poorly. We have little time remaining to mount this expedition."

"And where might that expedition be going?" asked Mouse.

"To the lost city of Falorn."

"The one in the Wailing Desert?"

"The same."

"Why does it wail?" Freya wondered, sotto voce.

"Later," Mouse replied from the corner of her mouth.

The advisor continued, ignoring the question. "There, our seekers will find a tomb, and retrieve a certain artefact."

"And what does the artefact do?"

"Nothing you need concern yourself with."

"There's undoubtedly a curse...?"

The round one roused himself at that. "If there is, I'll deal with it. It's unlikely to be beyond my abilities."

Freya raised an eyebrow. "*Unlikely*, or *impossible*?"

He frowned sourly, looking up to meet Freya's eyes. "*Impossible*, then." He didn't look away until the advisor cleared his throat.

Thomas tittered. "And anything he proves incapable of defeating? Well that will be mine to defeat."

"Well, then. *That's* reassuring."

The thin wizard blinked at Mouse, not sure whether he'd just been insulted.

"Enough. Follow Thomas and Mathias. They'll explain what you need to know of your expedition, and ensure that you're supplied. You leave on the morrow."

SWORDS & SORCERIES

*

Mathias provided horses, but warned they'd only carry the four adventurers to a border post at the edge of the Wailing Desert. Thereafter, they'd be given a suitable pack beast, but would need to walk; no riding animal could cross the sands or long survive the harsh desert conditions. Mouse vanished for a time, and returned with new clothing for herself and Freya: a loose, billowy head-to-toe garment, and a long, dirty-white hooded cloak.

They withdrew to a private room, removed all clothing save their small-clothes. Mouse held up her clothing. "The desert people call this garb a *thobe*, and the cloak, an *abernus*."

Freya held hers up sceptically; it would be a tight fit, whereas Mouse seemed like to disappear within her new clothing. "It seems fragile."

"The fabric is tough enough to endure harsh travel, but loose enough that air will pass freely through it and cool you. The cloak can cover your head and provide shelter from the sun by day and the cold by night."

"Deserts are cold at night?"

"You'd be amazed."

The roads around Losthaven were in good condition, and well patrolled against brigands, so they made good time. There was no conversation, each engaged in their own form of contemplation, whether mundane or mystical. At first, Thomas had essayed conversation with Mouse, but her acerbic tongue convinced him that his efforts would be futile. He considered engaging Freya, but her size frankly intimidated him. After a time, he frowned and began to complain to himself, at great length, in a low voice that held out until they reached the border post.

At the small, stockaded fort, Mathias presented a token to the commander, and the two withdrew to discuss their needs. While the men conferred, Mouse took Freya aside.

"What tribe are you from?"

"Pardon?"

"What tribe. I can't place your accent."

"Ah. No, I was born and raised in Losthaven. Unless Mother lied to me about my father, I'm as tender a shoot as ever sprang up amidst the cobblestones. And you? Which city did you spring from?"

Mouse snorted. "I grew up among a hill tribe two weeks' march from Losthaven. In fact, I never saw any settlement bigger than a clutch of peasant huts before this year."

The two women looked at each other, then shrugged simultaneously.

"Then I shall teach you the ways of civilized women."

"And I, in turn, shall teach you the ways of the barbarian."

"Deal." They shook hands, Freya being careful not to crush the smaller woman's hand, which was lost in hers. Mouse, unintimidated, returned her grip with commendable strength.

Entering the desert was like stepping across the threshold of a house: within the space of that one step (or two for Mouse), the vegetation changed from the lush fields and dense forest that surrounded Losthaven to bare rock and drifted sand.

"Is this natural?" wondered Freya aloud.

Mathias shook his head. "The desert was created by the last king of Falorn."

"Not intentionally," added Thomas.

"I've read that he was a powerful sorcerer, but perhaps less powerful than his wife, the queen."

The two mages exchanged glances. Thomas replied. "Nay, the stories of her power are greatly exaggerated. The King was the true source of power, and the true cause of his city's downfall. Now leave us in peace a moment while we confirm our path."

Freya whispered to Mouse. "A pleasant change. For once, they don't blame the woman."

Mouse spat on the rock. "That's as may be, but neither do they grant her any role."

"True. Are you surprised?"

"You could have knocked me over with a feather. One launched from an arbalest."

They exchanged cynical grins, and waited while the wizards conferred. The two men had drawn a map from its case, and stood shoulder to shoulder, holding opposite sides of the map. As they discussed, they looked to the sky and made occasional mystical gestures with a free hand.

Freya cleared her throat. "How will you know where we're going? I was given to understand that the lost city was... lost."

Mathias smiled up at her. "The explanation would be too mystical for a simple swordsman—swords*woman*—to understand. Suffice it to say that the relative locations of the planets, the moons, and the sun provide the necessary guidance. So long as we can see at least three of them simultaneously, with our eyes or more mystical tools, we can establish our position on this map to within the length of your small companion's sword. With four or more visible, we could determine our position within a finger's breadth." He rolled the map and tucked it away in its case. The end-cover closed with a loud snap. "We'd best be off."

The two mages led, followed by Freya with their pack animal, a strangely shaped beast with a foul temper and a tendency to spit gobs of thick cud at anyone who thwarted its desires. Mouse brought up the rear. The air was no hotter than in the lands around Losthaven, but was painfully dry, and the sun was intense. They were soon glad they'd packed as much water as their misshapen, hump-backed horse could carry. They were equally glad of the loose, flowing garments Mouse had procured. These wrapped around them and protected their face and eyes against both the sun and the stinging windblown sand. To the women's surprise, the two mages kept pace with them. It was only later, when the sound stopped, that they noticed the quiet chant the two men had been muttering as they walked, giving vigour to their strides.

That night, the four sat around a blazing campfire, which was rapidly consuming the small supply of firewood they'd loaded on the beast of burden. Around them, bare rock and lazily stirring sands stretched for miles.

Mouse sipped ale from a water skin. "Why do they call it the Wailing Desert?"

"Surely the winds?"

"No, Freya," Thomas replied. "Not the winds, else Losthaven would be found in the Wailing Grasslands beside the Wailing Forest and Wailing Lake."

"Why, then?"

Mathias gave them a sober look. "It's named for the ghosts of those who lived in Falorn before it was claimed by the desert."

"Ah."

Mouse snorted. "And they're wailing because they were too fat and slow to escape a moving desert?"

Mathias looked down at his broad midriff and frowned. "No. The desert took them overnight."

Freya thought a moment. "I'm no geomancer, but that seems fast for a desert."

The thin mage bestirred himself. "Blame their king. The most powerful spells don't always work out as planned, and there are consequences for failure." He tittered nervously, and missed the dark look his colleague shot him.

The women exchanged glances, and Freya inclined her head slightly. Mouse asked what they were both thinking. "So what do we seek, and how does it relate to this dead king?"

Mathias replied. "Our king, as you may know, claims descent from the kings of Falorn. Yet that descent, and by implication, his right to rule, has been called into question by the council. Should he be unable to prove that heritage, they'll remove him from the throne and replace him with a candidate more to the council's taste. We need you to keep us safe until we reach the crypt of the kings of Falorn, so we can retrieve the dead king's chain of office and return it to the living king."

"And that will be sufficient to prove that he's the legitimate ruler?"

"No one else will have the chain of office."

Mouse frowned. "So the chain of office represents the truth of the matter?"

"We shall convince them it's so."

Mouse's frown turned to a grin. "So if we kept the chain for ourselves, we'd then rule?"

Thomas shrank back under her fierce smile.

"Peace," said Freya. "Those who pay our wages decide what constitutes truth. And I've no desire to rule that pesthole of a city."

A chittering noise came from the darkness. Freya stood and drew her sword. "Is that the wailing you spoke of?"

Mouse rose, drawing her sword. "That's no ghost."

"What else is there to fear?"

"I don't know, but whatever it might be, it sounds large."

The two mages stepped behind the women and raised their hands, preparing their own, less visible, weapons.

The chittering drew nearer, and became a dim shadow at the edge of the firelight.

"Mouse? Follow my lead." Freya, eyes focused on the shadow, didn't look back to see whether her companion agreed.

All at once, in a rush of chitinous limbs, an enormous scorpion emerged from the darkness. It stood a good yard above the ground where its chelicerae joined its skull, but was at least four times that length, and its limbs clattered on the rock as it ran. Freya stepped between the enormous pincers and whipped her blade through a vertical arc that ended between its eyes with a *CLACK!*, stopping it momentarily in its tracks. She whipped her blade back up, barely in time to parry its stinger. Venom sprayed the rock behind her, and Mouse cursed.

Freya leapt backwards to avoid a second thrust. As she did, a small blur darted past her as Mouse lunged, stabbing the creature in one large eye. As Mouse recovered from her lunge, Freya slammed her blade against the pincer that tried to grab Mouse, redirecting that thrust downward. The scorpion's claw scraped across rock with a high-pitched squeal that made the women wince. Before Freya could try again to crush its head, Mouse lunged and blinded one of the secondary eyes.

The scorpion's chittering rose to ear-bleeding levels. It hesitated a moment, then turned and fled into the desert.

"We didn't kill it." Mouse sounded disappointed.

"Just as well," spoke Mathias, shuddering. "Its corpse would have attracted scavengers. We don't want to meet anything that would eat such a monstrosity."

"Best, then, that we maintain a careful watch, in case it returns."

The two mages nodded.

"And since we've done all the hard work thus far, I nominate you two seekers to take the first watch."

Seeing the look in her eyes, Thomas nodded.

*

The scorpion didn't return that night. The next morning, they shared a hasty, cold breakfast of biscuits and meat dried nearly hard as *cuir bouilli* armour, then set off farther into the desert. After a time, Mouse paused and cocked her head.

"We're being followed."

Freya looked at her. "You think?"

Mouse nodded. "Trust the barbarian."

"By what?"

"Were I to guess, I'd say a large predator."

Freya drew her sword. "Shall I go kill it?"

Mouse shook her head. "Wait. You'll just scare it off, and then it'll attack when we've forgotten it."

"Really?"

"Trust the barbarian."

"That seems the wise course. Unless..."

"Unless what?"

"Unless our two seekers have a better solution."

"Fair point." Freya cleared her throat. "Mathias! Thomas!"

The two mages stopped their muttering. "What?"

"We're being followed by some large predator. What can you do about that?"

The men exchanged glances. Thomas rolled up his

sleeves, and held his hands before his face, as if he were inspecting them. He flexed his fingers, cocked his hands, then spat a stream of liquid syllables. From behind a dune, there came the yowl of an enraged cat, loud enough to hurt the ears. The yowl vanished rapidly into the distance.

"Well done."

"It was nothing, Freya." Thomas giggled.

Mouse batted her eyes at her companion. "It was nothing, Freya," she whispered. The women exchanged grins, then resumed walking.

*

That night, as the women slept and the mages stood guard, the desert cat took their strange horse. Its screams woke them from their slumber. Before they could reach their feet, swords in hand, the cat was gone. They found only the two mages standing together, back to back within a glowing curved wall of light. The light from that wall danced upon the sand like sunlight on water.

"Where's our horse?"

The two men pointed into the darkness with trembling fingers.

Mouse kicked at their piled supplies. "At least we still have our supplies."

"That won't do us much good if we have to carry them ourselves."

"You can drop your shield, truth-seekers. The beast's long gone, and won't return before it's finished digesting its meal."

"You're sure?"

Mouse grunted. "Sure we shouldn't have left you two on watch."

"You'd have done better?"

"Couldn't have done worse now, could we?"

The men glared at Mouse.

Freya cleared her throat. "That's not productive. I don't suppose you two have any way to summon a mystical beast of burden to carry all of this for us?" She paused. "Didn't think so. Very well. In the morning, you two will carry the food. I'll carry the water, and Mouse will keep an eye out for any other hungry fellow travellers. In the meantime, get some sleep in case Mouse was wrong and the cat returns. We'll stand watch."

*

By morning, the cat hadn't returned. Freya kicked sand into the mages' faces to wake them.

"Time to get moving."

Grumbling and wiping their eyes, they rose from the sand and walked a discreet distance into the dunes. When they returned, Freya and Mouse set about dividing the load as best they could. Then they shared a silent and hasty breakfast. As on previous days, the mages conferred over their map, then agreed upon their direction and prepared to set off.

"Drink deep now, then refill your bottle from the water skins." Mouse took her own advice, and the others followed. Then they each shouldered their burdens, Freya grunting under the weight of the water skins.

Freya shrugged her broad shoulders to settle the load. "How far are we from the ruins?"

"Less than a day. With luck, we'll arrive before noon."

They travelled, uneventfully, as the sun rose in the sky, and not long after it began its descent, Falorn came into view, nearly submerged under the sands that lapped against the walls like waves against a sinking lifeboat. Only the palace, or what remained of it, rose high above the encroaching sands.

"Transient are the works of man," Mathias announced, with some satisfaction. "We'll camp beneath the walls. We should be safe from the ghosts."

"*Should* be," Thomas replied.

Mathias nodded. "We'll wait until morning to enter the city. The light will be better, and the ghosts quieter."

They stopped a spear-throw from the walls, in the lee of the city, where they found the best shelter against the blowing sand. Freya dropped their water skins with a groan and sat heavily. As the sun continued its descent, the wind stilled, to be replaced by a faint keening from within the walls. As darkness fell, the keening increased in volume to become full-blown wailing, and the women tried, without much success, to plug their ears against the sound.

Mouse noticed the two men seemed unaffected. "*Hey, seekers*! How is it the caterwauling doesn't bother you?"

Mathias apologized. "Forgive us." He made a gesture with his left hand, and hissed a word that hung upon the air before dispersing. Instantly, the wailing ceased.

Freya glanced around nervously. "Did you banish them?"

"Nay, I merely muted them for a time."

"And I'll keep them from disturbing our sleep." Thomas pulled a short length of polished blonde wood from his sleeve and walked a circle around their camp, dragging the wand behind him and muttering under his breath. In his wake, a transparent curtain sprang up that glowed faintly. When he'd completed the circle, the curtain flared once, then vanished. Later, as full darkness fell, grey, transparent human shapes appeared, walking listlessly from the city towards them. There were men and women, children and stooped ancients, and they wore tattered rags, as if time and windblown sand had eaten at their clothing. Their faces and skin were desiccated and shrunken, as if the dry desert air had sucked all the moisture from them.

The invisible curtain kept them at bay, but they circled the camp, mouths open as if they were wailing — or trying to say something. But whatever Mathias had done, it silenced their voices. As the ghosts circled the camp, kept out by the invisible wall, they gazed hopelessly at the travellers. Their eyes were disturbing voids that plucked at one's eyes, and even the wizards would not meet that gaze. The ghosts continued their hopeless circling of the camp all night, leaving only as the sun rose above the horizon.

After a light breakfast, the four refilled their water bottles, covered the rest of their supplies with a blanket whose edges they weighted down with sand, and walked to the city walls. In the lee, the walls rose well above their head. But upwind the sand had overtopped the walls and fallen on the far side, creating an easy scramble up and a steeper slope down the other side. They descended in swooping steps, sand giving way beneath their feet and turning each step into a slide of several feet.

"This way," Thomas said, and led them towards the palace without hesitation. They entered, then walked through sand-choked corridors to a flight of stone stairs that descended steeply into the ground. There, he snapped his fingers, and a glowing light appeared above and slightly before his head. Mathias conjured his own light, then both swept down the stairs.

Freya looked at Mouse. "I suppose we're obligated to follow our truth-seekers."

Mouse looked at Freya. "I suppose we are. At least, if we hope to travel in the light."

Freya bowed and swept an arm gracefully before her. "After you, Milady!"

Mouse curtsied, then grinned and followed the mages. They descended perhaps a hundred feet into the ground, careful to keep within the area lit by the mages' lights, each footstep dislodging a choking cloud of dust. When they reached the bottom, they followed the trail the two mages had broken through the dust, eventually arriving at a crypt with many burial niches along walls that receded into the darkness. A rune-covered sarcophagus stood at the room's centre.

"Uncover it, Freya," commanded Thomas.

*

Mathias stepped beyond his puddle of urine, withdrew a wand from his cloak, and levelled it at the spirit.

"Do you really think that wise?"

He looked up at Freya. "Keep to subjects you understand, giantess, and leave magic to its masters."

Freya shrugged and stepped back.

The wand's tip glowed, and Mathias stood straighter and with more intensity than he'd shown before. "I charge you, begone!"

The spectre laughed, and made a brushing-aside motion. The wand flew into the darkness beyond the diminished circle of light. Mathias made a choking noise, then raised his arms above his head, as if warding off some crushing force. As the women watched, he gradually bent under that invisible pressure, pressed relentlessly downward until, with a groan, he slumped to the ground. The light faded, replaced by the dim glow of the blank-eyed ghost that rose from his corpse. With a despairing wail, it fled into the darkness, leaving the two women in the dark.

The king's voice filled the darkness. "That leaves only you two."

Freya cleared her throat, which had gone suddenly dry. "If it please you, your highness, might there be light so we can see you and plead our case?"

"That seems only fair." Golden light fell from the stone ceiling, revealing the corpse and the cinders. Mouse took a step farther from the pool of urine beside the corpse.

Freya took a deep breath. "We're here at the behest of your descendent, the King of Losthaven."

The spectre crossed its arms on its chest. "I know nothing of this city. Tell me more."

Freya explained the situation concisely. "So you see, sire, we're here to retrieve your chain of office and return it to Losthaven to restore legitimacy to your descendant's reign."

"I see. And you think a piece of clanky metal will do that?"

"I wouldn't venture to speculate. I was merely paid to return the chain. What happens thereafter is their problem."

Mouse frowned. "*Will be paid*, she means. Without the chain, there'll be no payment."

The spectre laughed. "*That* is not *my* problem. But I confess, being confined within these walls weighs upon one. And I feel some curiosity about the fate of my descendants." He paused a moment in thought. "Very well." He gestured at the sarcophagus with one wispy hand. "Gather my bones, and the chain you seek. Carry me to this Losthaven of yours."

"And me."

The two women jumped. A second spectre had appeared, wearing a tiara upon its forehead. Freya leaned forward to glance into the sarcophagus. "Two skulls."

"Indeed. Our last command to our followers before they fled the encroaching desert was that we be interred together for eternity."

"How romantic."

The queen frowned. "There are some thoughts you should keep to yourself, small one. In the meantime, have we a bargain?"

Mouse stood a little straighter. "And what shall our reward be?"

"Whatever you negotiated with our descendant, that shall be yours. In addition, you may keep whatever there is of value from our sarcophagus, save only our crowns and rings."

"Including the chain?"

"Including the chain. The power of command inheres in the wearer, not the chain."

The women exchanged glances, then Freya removed her cloak, and began gently transferring bones to it. When she'd wrapped the bones, the spectres sank into the cloak and disappeared, though their faint illumination persisted. She examined the sarcophagus. Little remained.

"I should know better than to trust a king's word." She sighed and reached into the sarcophagus once more. All that remained were two ornate knives with jewelled hilts, two woven silver belts, and a silver sceptre that she gave to Mouse for safekeeping.

They ascended the stairs slowly, relying only on the faint light from the bones.

*

"You're *sure* you know where you're going?"

"Trust the barbarian."

"I've *trusted the barbarian* for three days. I now have sand in every crevice of my body, including places best not mentioned. It only took us two days to reach the city. It's a well-known fact that the return journey is always shorter than the outbound travel. Ergo..."

Mouse sighed. "Ergo, we must be lost."

"That seems the logical interpretation."

"I blame these shifting sands. In a civilized wilderness, the landmarks stay in place, allowing reliable navigation."

Freya snorted and dropped the water skins she'd been carrying. With two fewer members of their expedition, there'd originally been ample water for the women, but her burden had shrunk alarmingly during the three days of their wandering. "Still, whatever the merits of *civilized* wilderness, it seems we may need more assistance than your barbarian instincts have provided here in its uncivilized cousin."

Mouse blinked. "I have a thought." She placed the cloak containing the bones upon the sand and cleared her throat. "Your highnesses?"

After a moment, twin black clouds rose from the bones, resolving into the forms of the king and his queen. They looked around, blinking in the intense light.

The king spoke first. "Are we there yet? Ah, I see we aren't. What seems to be the problem, giantess?"

"Our navigation skills."

"I'm grateful for the *our*."

"Don't mention it."

The King cleared his throat warningly. "So you two are lost?"

"Quite thoroughly."

The queen replied. "And you want us to save you?"

"If it wouldn't be too much trouble. Your former tomb

undoubtedly felt more confining than this vast expanse of sky, but if we don't escape this desert, you'll find yourself longing for the comforts of the tomb after a few centuries of burial beneath the sands."

"You have a point." The queen closed her eyes a moment, then pointed. "That way. About three days."

The living women exchanged glances.

"No," continued the queen. "We cannot transport you. You'll have to walk."

"Needs must," sighed Freya, and shouldered what remained of the water.

*

By the second day, their water was gone. Freya spat grit from her dry mouth. "You should ride upon my shoulders."

"Won't that tire you faster?"

Freya snorted. "My water skin weighs more than you. *Weighed* more than you."

"That's because you're freakishly large and carry a proportionally excessive amount of water."

"There's no denying that."

Mouse heard the implied *but*. "But?"

Freya sighed. "When my limbs eventually fail me and I fall, then you'll still be fresh, and can carry on in search of water. I trust that, as the barbarian among us, you'll find water and bring enough back to revive me."

Mouse's lips quirked a grin. "I shall endeavour to be worthy of your trust."

"Best you be. Or you'll be dealing with a large and thirsty ghost for the rest of your undoubtedly short life."

"Even the heroic heart quails at that prospect. Very well, then." Freya knelt, and Mouse climbed upon her shoulders.

*

In the event, they escaped the desert before such desperate measures became necessary, though Freya was staggering before they crossed into wetter lands. At the border post, they rehydrated for a day, then took horse for Losthaven, and arrived in good time.

"You took long enough," complained the advisor, scowling down his nose at Mouse and then up his nose at Freya. "And what have you done with my sorcerers?"

"Your sorcerers chose to be rude to the king of Falorn, who taught them the importance of politesse."

"Wait—there's a king in Falorn?"

"No," said the dead king, rising from Freya's bundled cloak, accompanied by his queen. "There's a king in *Losthaven.*"

The advisor blanched.

"And it's our first desire that you pay these two women the sum you agreed upon", added the queen.

Hands shaking, the advisor withdrew a large bag of coins from a pocket of his robes, and tossed it to Mouse. Mouse made it disappear.

The Queen smiled a cold smile that had not been warmed in the least by the desert sun. "You have our permission to leave, warriors. And our gratitude for bringing us here. Now, *you: advisor.* Bring us to our descendent and his council. We have the matter of his legitimacy to discuss."

Freya and Mouse left the audience chamber with alacrity.

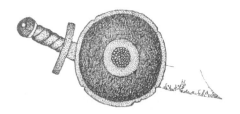

DISRUPTION OF DESTINY
Gerri Leen

Isabel examined the stripling plant, poking shallow holes around it to help it grow better and let air get to the roots. She looked down the row of older plants; several were dying. It depressed her to think of pulling them out—it was the nature of things to pass away, but such a visible reminder of the impermanence of life always made her sad.

She heard hoof beats in the distance but kept to her work as the sound grew louder. A large group of riders came into view, dressed in full battle gear, shields and swords rattling as they rushed by her, heading south. A new warlord was active but she hadn't paid much attention. As long as he stayed in the south, she wouldn't worry about him

Her bones creaked as she stood up. She was old: her knees told her so, as did her back when the rains threatened. New pains seemed to erupt each morning as she struggled out of bed—an ache here, a sharp shooting pain there. Her herbs and potions could barely keep up with them.

She'd lived a long life and knew she would live a few more years. The cards never lied to her. Neither did the lines on her palms or the stars in the sky. If you knew how to read the signs, the future was clear. She would die old, but she wouldn't die ancient.

She felt something brush against her skirt and looked down. Grisca meowed a greeting. Her plush grey coat was covered with dust and bits of leaves. Stooping to brush her off, Isabel ignored the pain that shot through her back as she moved. "Where have you been? You know I need you here when I work."

The cat mewed, a conciliatory tone in the cry.

"Yes, I know it's not fair to expect you to stay in the house all the time. But you could at least be close by. It's been two days since I've seen you." She picked a burr from the cat's tail, then let her hand rest on the animal's soft head. She could feel the purr begin, rumbling from deep within Grisca, then pouring out as pure energy through Isabel's hand, filling her old body with strength.

She straightened and there was no pain. When Grisca wanted to be helpful, she was exceedingly so. "Thank you, love. Let's make some tea. Before our visitor arrives."

Isabel bustled around the stillroom, found the herbs she wanted, and carried them to the main room to steep in a pot. Setting her best candlestick on the table, she brought out her small box of candles. White for purity? Yellow for creativity? She dug deeper and found the dark crimson candle—the best one for protection. She set it in the candlestick, pushing it down securely so it wouldn't fall over.

Grisca leapt up on the table, batting at the deck of cards that sat waiting. She seemed unusually interested in this visitor.

"Not yet. You know that."

The cat jumped down, disappearing into the stillroom. If Grisca had hands instead of paws, she probably could have done all the prep work herself, might even be able to carry on Isabel's work once her life was over, but alas. Following the cat into the stillroom, Isabel picked out some aromatic herbs and began to pound them into a powder. She added less pleasant ingredients, crushing them so they'd blend with the aromatics. Her hands ached as she used the pestle to grind the roots and leaves into the same fine powder as the rest. When she was younger, she could grind a mortar twice this size and not give it a second thought. But now she had to rest frequently as her hands seized up with cramp.

Grisca cried softly.

"Oh, I'm all right," Isabel said. The cat had no idea what it was like to get old; she'd shown up on Isabel's porch sixty years before, looking just as she did now—she hadn't aged a day since then.

Grisca turned and walked into the hallway, stopping at the closed door and sniffing. Isabel turned away, not wanting to look at the door, not wanting to be reminded.

The cat meowed.

"I'm busy. If you want in, get in. But I'll not help you when I'm working."

The cat meowed again, then ran back out to the main room. A few moments later, Isabel saw her through the window, crossing the grass toward the stable. Grisca leapt up to the top of the fence as Tremaud appeared. The great white stallion seemed to float rather than walk into the sunshine. His coat gleamed like new-fallen snow from the brushing Isabel had given him earlier. He gently nosed Grisca, and the cat leapt to his back, where she sat on velvet paws while the horse took her for a tour of the small paddock.

Isabel smiled and turned back to her powder; it was ready. She poured a small amount of wine into a wooden chalice, then added the powder to the wine, stirring carefully until the herbs were completely dissolved. She set the goblet on a high shelf where it would soak in the sun's rays. Later, the wine would bathe in the light of the moon.

Satisfied that she was done, Isabel sat down at her table and lit the candle with a taper from the fire. Pouring herself a cup of tea, she waited.

She was dozing, Grisca curled at her feet, when the sound of footsteps coming up the stone walk roused her.

"Hello?" a man called out.

Isabel smiled. He was here.

She turned, looking up at the man who stood in her doorway. Loomed in it, actually—his sturdy body filled the entire space. He moved, and a soft clinking sound accompanied his motion as the links of chain mail he wore over his tunic rubbed gently against each other. Coins— silver, she expected, for he didn't look well-heeled enough to carry gold—tinkled in his purse. He wore a scabbard from which a fine sword projected. A gemstone, deep red, was set in the pommel. On his other hip, he wore a duelling dagger; its elaborately carved handle gleamed even in the low light.

She gestured for him to come in. "What can I do for you, warrior?"

"I was told you could see the future?"

"The future, the past, the present. Are you sure the future is what you're most concerned with?"

He looked at her for a moment, then looked away. She realized he was much younger than he appeared.

"You've fought in many battles. They've changed you. Scarred you."

"Yes." He moved toward her table. "What can you tell me of that?"

"You've seen too much blood." She studied him. "Too much carnage. Been a cause of much of it. You question your life."

He nodded. "Yes, I'm heartsick."

"Soulsick more like." She gestured to the other chair. "Sit down, sir."

"Please, my name is Leopold."

"And I'm Isabel."

"It's a pleasure." He smiled, and the expression made him look much younger.

She had the feeling he didn't smile often. "What's gone wrong in your life, Leopold?"

He looked away and sighed, as if unwilling to share his secrets.

Grisca jumped on the table, nosing his hand. He petted her absently, and Isabel could hear the cat purring from where she sat.

"You cannot say?" she finally asked as Leopold continued to pet her cat. "Or you will not?"

He looked at her startled.

She smiled gently. "I don't judge. And, in any case, I've only to ask these"—she picked the cards up and tapped them on the table—"to find out the truth."

"They hold my future?"

"They tell of your future. It's a slightly different thing. The future is dependent on your actions now and in the past."

"Is that true? I can change my future by what I do now?" He seemed very excited by the idea.

"To an extent you can change the small details as the waves can change the pattern in the sand. But your destiny is written in firmer material."

"Like rock," he said, his face falling. "I don't like destiny."

"Is your destiny so bad?" She indicated the stone at the end of his sword, then the fancy dagger. "You appear to have done well by it. I know your shirt is of costly material that sheds water and keeps you warm. I know in your purse you carry coins that buy you a hot meal and a soft bed when you need those things. You haven't known poverty in a long time."

"This is true. But I would give it all up."

"Why?"

He sighed. "A soft bed and a hot meal cannot erase what I've seen and done. The lives that I've taken can never be given back."

"Did you kill in anger?"

"Of course not."

She smiled softly. "In vengeance, then? Or for profit?"

"No. I fight for justice, for a better world."

"Then you have nothing to regret, Leopold," she said gently.

"It's not regret, exactly. I'm just..."

"Tired?"

"Yes. I'm very tired." He looked down again. "There's a warlord to the south. He's terrorizing the villagers, and I am on my way to join the forces that fight him. It will be a long siege because he's gone to ground in his fortress. I'm needed, but...I don't want to go." His face turned red midway through his story, his skin darkening the more he spoke.

She realized it wasn't easy for him to say these things. "What would you rather do?"

He looked past her, his gaze so far away she wondered where he had gone. Finally, he spoke, and his voice was hushed, as if he was offering her a prayer. "I wish to retire. To have a family — a wife who'll smile when we wake in the morning, children who'll run to me when they see me. I'd like to have a home with land that I can farm. Something to call my own."

She smiled. "It's a beautiful dream."

"I want it to be more than a dream. I want it to be my life."

She could feel her smile fading. "It will never happen, Leopold."

"Why not?"

She pulled out the cards and handed them to him. "Pick two."

He pulled two cards from the deck.

"Turn them over."

He had chosen the Ten of Swords and the Death card.

"A warrior's death. Violent. Bloody."

He went white.

She took the cards back up, shuffled thoroughly, and held the deck out again. "Pick another two, lay them out."

He did so. They were the same two cards. He knocked them off the table, and Grisca began to play with them. Shooing her away, Isabel rescued the cards.

"A witch's tricks," he muttered.

"Not at all. It's your destiny. You're a warrior; you'll fight and you'll die a violent death. It's written in the stars, in the lines on your palms, in the story the cards will tell of you. You can't change your destiny."

"I do not want this destiny."

"I believe you. But your destiny has been with you since you were born to this earth. It won't go away simply because you wish it to."

He slapped his hands down hard on the table, causing the cards and the candle to jump. "I'll do more than just wish it. I'll walk away. I won't fight anymore."

"And that might work for a while. But eventually a moment will come when you'll have to choose to fight or not. And you will fight. You're a warrior; your first reaction will be to reach for your sword."

"I'll sell my sword." His voice was surly, like a small boy who knew he was fighting a losing battle with his mother.

"Then you'll reach for a stake, or a scythe, or a stout beam. You will fight, Leopold, because it's in your nature to fight. And it's in your nature, because it's your destiny."

He slumped, looking defeated.

She leaned forward and touched his hand. "There is another way."

He slowly looked up.

"You can't wish it away. You can't run from it. But you can give it away...to me. I know a spell."

"Give you my destiny?"

She nodded. "If you truly want a new life, I can give you that. I just can't guarantee what kind of life that will be."

He shook his head; he didn't understand.

She sighed. "You have one true destiny, Leopold. One path that's yours to follow through life. If I take that from you, you won't be the same. You'll be changed utterly."

"Changed how?"

"You'll be..." She searched for the right word. "Empty. Missing something."

"Not my soul?" He seemed to be reaching for his sword.

"Easy, my friend. I'm not the devil, nor do I wish to take your soul." Shaking her head, she tried to think of a better way to explain it. "Have you ever seen a man who's bumped his head hard and afterward cannot remember who he is or where he comes from?"

"Yes, of course."

"And sometimes, those men can remember things in the far past, but not what they had to eat the day before."

"Yes, I've seen that."

"It will be a bit like that."

"Will I be some sort of idiot?"

"No, not at all. What I mean is that, for a time, there will be gaps. You won't remember things. Like fighting, for instance."

He seemed to think about that. "So all my life that has to do with fighting—"

"Will be gone, yes. Over time, new experiences will fill in the gaps."

"And I'll make my own destiny?" His eyes shone.

"Not exactly. You see, the gods don't like emptiness. If you don't have a destiny, one will find you. And there's no way of knowing what it will be. You could die of the plague in a year, or you might live to be an old man with grandchildren toddling around your knees. There's no way to predict."

"Can't your cards tell us what would happen?"

"No," she said. "They can only see your destiny as it is now, your true destiny. So long as it's with you, they can't see beyond it. Until you give it away, we won't know what will befall you."

He sighed, and Grisca nosed him again, mewing slightly at Isabel, who patted his hand.

"You don't have to decide right now," she said. "Go away and think about it. I'll be here whenever you're ready."

He seemed grateful for the reprieve, nodding slowly as if in great thought. He rose and walked to the door, then turned. "What will you do with my destiny?"

She smiled gently as she stood. "I will put it in an empty place where it will run its course and then die at the appointed time."

He frowned and looked down. "Do you know when that is? Can you see when I will die?"

She was about to answer when he held up his hand.

"No, don't tell me. I don't want to know." He touched his dagger, as if the shiny metal brought him some kind of comfort. "If I do this, I want it to be because I'm walking toward something good, not running away from death. I don't seek this so that I can live a self-indulgent life, you know?"

"You still want to help people?"

He nodded. "Just perhaps in a less bloody way?"

She was impressed by his words, his courage. He was a

champion, not just a warrior. "Go and consider your future, Leopold. The world has need of its warriors. Maybe it's not right for you to cast your destiny aside."

"Perhaps not." He dug into his purse.

She shook her head. "Payment isn't necessary."

"Not until I decide?"

She smiled, a small steely smile. "Not even then."

He stared at her, his eyes cool and considering. "Why do you do this, then, if not for payment?"

"I had a son. Willem. He was a warrior like you. Ripe with destiny. I knew his future, knew he would fight into old age. He would train other warriors and lead them into glorious and righteous battle. I saw it all for him. And I was proud. No mother was ever prouder. No mother ever loved her son more."

She could feel tears starting and blinked furiously, dashing them back. "One day, he fought a wizard and hurt him badly. On his deathbed, the wizard cursed him— changing his destiny—and I lost my Willem. Long before his time." She could feel her chin trembling and bit down hard, determined to control it.

"I'm sorry."

She nodded. "I couldn't change Willem's destiny. But I can change yours. If you want me to."

He didn't answer. She realized there was a new look in his eyes—one she wasn't sure she liked. Pity.

She stood straighter. "I have medicines to mix, Leopold. You can let yourself out?"

She turned away, walking quickly to the stillroom. Her eyes were caught by the closed door in the hall. Willem's door. She touched it and felt the hum of magic. She'd left it just the way he liked it. No dust, no decay could get through the web of protection she and Grisca had woven around his room. Only they could get through.

She often found Grisca on Willem's bed, as if—

Isabel forced herself not to think of Willem. She must be ready. She had potions to mix. And a spell to perform when Leopold chose to cast aside his destiny. She could see him walking—he appeared to be deep in thought. But she knew he'd be back. They always came back.

*

The next morning, Isabel rose early. She wasn't surprised to see Tremaud standing in the paddock, waiting for her. He nickered softly as she came close.

"Hello, boy." She caressed his soft neck, rubbing the space between his eyes as he lowered his head, giving her more access.

She'd never loved a horse more than this one. Willem's horse, his battle stallion. Now out to pasture. But still powerful, still strong. Still a warhorse at heart and in body. She kept him that way. She was too old to ride, but not too old to lunge him. Grisca often sat on his back like a circus acrobat as the horse cantered around Isabel in the fields. For all his mighty power, the stallion was docile around her. She knew her magic had a lot to do with that. Animals responded to it better than most people did.

She poured out oats for Tremaud, a special meal. He moved in eagerly, and she left him eating.

Grisca sat on the threshold, by the small flowerpots that never seemed to bloom right. Isabel refused to use magic on them, wanting something in her life to be normal, natural— not dependent on the arts that had been strong in her since she was a child.

The flowers might have been happier if she'd used spells

on them. They always seemed to lack water and took in too much sun. Grisca jumped into one of the pots and nosed the flower as if in disdain.

"No magic, Grisca."

The cat jumped out and walked away toward the stable, clearly offended.

Isabel didn't react. Grisca would be back. When it was time to work the magic, she would return.

"Hello," Leopold called from the road, riding a beautiful chestnut mare.

Tremaud nickered to the mare and bucked, and Isabel smiled at the stallion's antics in front of such a comely visitor.

Jumping down, Leopold strode toward her eagerly. "I've made up my mind."

She waited.

He laughed and looked up at the sky. "I want to be free. I want to live my own life, whatever that means. Take my destiny away from me. Please?"

"How can you be sure?"

He smiled; he seemed to be remembering something. "I just am."

"Leopold, this isn't like taking away a sore throat. This is very serious work. Tell me why I should do this for you?"

"I fell in love this morning."

She knew her look was rife was disbelief.

He only laughed. "Her name is Marthe. Do you know her?"

The widow on the far side of town. As comely as Leopold's mare, and probably just as attractive to him as his lovely chestnut was to Tremaud. "Yes, I know her. A sweet woman. And a sad one. Her husband died after only a few months of marriage, leaving her to try to farm the land without him."

"Yes. She told me this." He blushed. "I went out early this morning, thinking to clear my head with a ride on Casha. When I rode past her farm, Marthe was in the road, struggling to fix a fence post that had fallen in. I helped her. And she gave me water and some breakfast." He sighed. "She's so brave."

Isabel couldn't hide her smile. "And you desire her?"

"I do. And I could be of great help to her." He looked down. "Except that she must have thought me an imbecile. I was so taken with her that I could barely stammer out my name. For the most part, I just listened to her." He shook his head. "She'll never think me worthy of her interest."

Isabel laughed softly. "You're handsome and strong. That can make up for many flaws."

"Do you think so?"

She nodded. "You're walking toward something, Leopold. Not away. That is good."

"So you'll do it?"

"I will."

"Can you do it now?"

"Yes," she said, her voice barely more than a whisper.

"Then do it. Please. I can't stand to wait a moment longer."

"All right. Come in."

He followed her inside, and she relit the crimson candle, indicating he should sit while she went to the stillroom. Grisca appeared as if from nowhere, mewing with anticipation.

"Must I prepare in some way?" Leopold asked from the other room.

"If there's any doubt in your mind, you must make peace with it. You must be absolutely sure this is what you want, or the spell won't work."

Grisca meowed.

Isabel laughed softly. The cat understood men too well. "Yes, if he just thinks of Marthe, he won't be able to remember his doubts."

She didn't think they'd have to encourage him to focus on Marthe. Leopold would be able to think of little else. He was in the first flush of enchantment. Not by magic, though. By a force just as old. Attraction. Desire. Love.

She sighed. It had been years since she'd even thought of such things. She could barely remember how it had been with Pieter and her, when they'd first come together so many years ago. Her husband had died the year after Willem was born. He'd barely known his son before he was taken by a fever that had swept through the area. She'd loved him intensely. Now she could scarcely remember what that had felt like.

She hoped Leopold fared better in his quest for love.

Reaching up, she took down the goblet. The powder had separated slightly, so she stirred the mixture gently. She grabbed a velvet bag from another shelf, then carried it and the goblet out to the table.

Leopold smiled at her, his eyes shining with hope and determination.

"No doubts?" she asked.

"None." His smile grew bigger.

She untied the velvet bag and held it out to him, high enough so he couldn't see what was inside. "Reach in and pick one of the stones."

He drew out the garnet. It gleamed, catching the firelight, and the stone in his sword echoed it.

She smiled—it was a perfect selection. The fates approved, or at least wouldn't interfere in her magic. She handed him the goblet.

"It's important that you think of Marthe as you drink. Don't think of anything else. Just remember all the things she told you—remember how she makes you feel. Can you do that?"

He nodded, his smile shyly embarrassed. "I can think of little else."

"Then drink all of this. And concentrate." She sat down across from him.

He closed his eyes, a slow smile crossing his face as he picked up the goblet. He drained it slowly.

She caught the goblet as he slumped forward, his head falling dangerously close to the candle, his hair starting to singe. Pushing the candle away from him, Isabel looked down at the goblet. Inside—invisible to anyone who couldn't see the magic—was his destiny. If she held the goblet to his lips, his destiny would go rushing back to him. She stood, covered the goblet with a white cloth, and set it on the mantle.

Grisca leapt on the table, staring intently at Leopold. Isabel often wondered if the cat could see the new destiny filling these tired champions they helped. When Grisca gave a short meow and jumped down, Isabel touched Leopold's head, gently pushing him.

He sat up slowly, rubbing his eyes. "Where am I?"

She smiled. "You came in here to have your fortune read." She gestured at the cards. "But you said you felt faint. Don't you remember?"

He frowned, obviously trying to remember. Then he shook his head. "I don't remember much."

"Do you remember who you are?"

"My name is Leopold and I'm a..." His frown grew deeper. "I'm..." He looked up at her. "I don't know what I do, how I make my living."

"You told me that you wished to learn to farm. There's a place on the far side of town you said you'd visited."

His expression lightened. "Yes. Marthe's place. I remember Marthe." He laughed and seemed more confident. "Of course, I'm Leopold. I'm a farmer. Or I'm going to be?"

"I think you're going to be." She touched the fine sword, then moved her hand over to the dagger. "You can sell those, you know. They'll fetch a pretty pile of silver."

He nodded.

"And you've a horse out there. Her saddle is worth a great deal."

He frowned. "I don't know why I have these things."

"Perhaps a relative left them to you?"

"That's possible. Yes."

"If you decide you want to sell them, Mister Waring will give you a good price for them. He's an honest man."

He seemed touched that she would think of him. "Thank you. I'm afraid I don't remember your name?"

"It's Isabel."

"Isabel. I don't think I want my fortune read." He laughed uncomfortably. "If I've wasted your time, I'm sorry."

She smiled. "It's of no concern. It was pleasant talking with you. I don't get many visitors this far out of town."

He stood up, and she walked him to the door. He looked around at the fields that stretched until they met the forest. "You're very isolated here."

"I like it that way."

He turned to her. "If you ever have need of me...?"

It was her turn to be touched. Some men were champions even without their destinies. "I'll remember to call for you. Good fortune to you, Leopold. I hope life brings you only good things."

She could tell he was thinking of Marthe as he smiled broadly.

"Well, goodbye," he said. He walked up to the horse and mounted her awkwardly. "Is she even mine?"

"Oh, I think she is. See how still she stands for you?"

He touched her red mane tentatively.

"Her name is Casha. Or so you said when you rode up." She pointed to where Tremaud was still watching the mare. "I remember because my stallion seems to have developed quite a fancy for her."

Leopold's instincts for riding appeared to take over—his legs hung more naturally, his hands as they took up the reins were more sure. "I think I could breed horses," he said, as if on the verge of a great discovery.

"I imagine you could. I'd be happy to offer Tremaud's services." She looked back at the stallion. "He'd be happy to be offered."

Leopold laughed. A giddy, unaffected sound. "I'll let you know. Good bye, Isabel."

She held her hand up and watched him race down the road until he was out of sight, and the dust cloud Casha had kicked up had settled back to the ground. Then she turned and went back into the house.

She took a deep breath and sat down at the table. Her heart pounded strangely. Spells like this weren't easy any longer. As Leopold had drunk the wine, she'd felt the magic tugging at her, making her reach deep into the earth to reinforce her power.

She wondered how many more times she could do this. Would she get too old, too frail, to properly channel the power?

She looked up at the goblet. She must let the destiny settle a bit, the same way the dust on the road had settled.

As she waited, she let her eyes close.
Tired. She was so tired.

*

Waking slowly, Isabel saw that the candle had nearly burned down—she'd been asleep for almost two hours.

She looked at the goblet. It was ready.

Forcing herself to her feet, she picked up the goblet. She could feel Leopold's destiny held safely inside by her magic. Destiny—waiting to be used, to be poured into an empty place.

She walked to Willem's room, touching the door, the tracings of magic parting to let her in. Grisca ran in from the outside and followed her into the room.

Moving to Willem's bed, Isabel saw the indentation from where the cat had last slept—right next to his chin.

Her Willem's chin. He lay silent as ever on the bed. His eyes staring sightlessly. Lost. He was lost.

The wizard had cursed well. Live, he'd shouted to the winds, raining his curse down on Willem as her son waited outside the stronghold for a battle that was never to take place.

Live, the wizard had said. Live forever. Be young and strong forever. And do nothing, know nothing, feel nothing. Forever.

Her Willem. Alive. Forever. In this husk that wouldn't age, wouldn't weaken or waste away. Young and strong and beautiful. In the first flush of youth's prime. Like the day he'd set out to fight the wizard. Forty years ago.

"I have something for you, my son. A little gift."

Grisca jumped up next to him and nosed him softly.

"You know, if I could, I'd give you back your own

destiny. But the best I can do is give you someone else's." Isabel held the goblet to his lips, and Leopold's destiny poured into Willem.

She pulled the goblet away and set it aside. Grisca crawled onto Willem's chest and pushed her head under his chin as she purred.

Willem began to stir, then his eyes opened, and he looked up at her in confusion. "Didn't it work?" he asked in Leopold's voice.

"Give it a moment." She waited.

It would take time to integrate the new destiny — it always did.

"I feel so strange." Willem closed his eyes. Then he opened them again, and smiled at her. Her son's bright, open smile. "Mother? Did I oversleep?"

"Just a bit."

He scratched Grisca's chin. "Hello, you."

The cat began to purr even louder.

Isabel looked up, forcing away the tears that came with each new awakening. Willem didn't know how he spent most of his days. No one knew. She'd kept it from the world all these years, only telling those men who would give her their destinies the truth — that he was lost. The townspeople thought he lived far away, that the boy who came to visit her every so often was her grandson. He never stayed awake long enough for anyone in town to speak to him, to realize the truth.

And Willem himself seemed to have little idea of how much time had passed. Someday, he might understand the strangeness of his existence. When the methods of fighting had changed, when the world had passed him by. But for now, he was just another warrior, another champion, roaming the countryside in search of injustice to fight.

Something he could do as long as she was alive and able to wield the magic.

She didn't like to contemplate what would happen to him once she was dead. She wished she could enchant herself so that she could care for him forever, but every time she tried, she failed.

Willem gently pushed Grisca off his chest and swung his legs out of bed with hearty gusto. "I must be off. There's a warlord to the south who's terrorizing the villagers."

She nodded. If Leopold wouldn't live out his destiny, then someone must. "Tremaud is ready for you. I brushed him out yesterday. Your travel gear is all packed."

A more benign variation of the wizard's curse had worked to keep Willem's war stallion young and strong. Isabel often thought she should feel guilty, but found it impossible to regret doing it. The horse had carried her lifeless yet somehow still living son back to her after the wizard cursed him, and he would carry him again if Willem died in battle. If they both died, the spellmark she had tattooed on her son's head and on Tremaud's inner flank would bring them home whether they willed it or not.

Her spell would bring Tremaud back to life, just as the wizard's curse would bring her son back to non-life...to wait. For the next time—the next destiny. Over and over until there could be no next time—until she was dead. She didn't know if her spell on Tremaud would endure the way the curse on her son had survived when the wizard died, but she prayed to whatever god would listen to her that it would. She couldn't imagine her Willem without his beloved horse.

Leaving Willem to put on his battle gear, she packed a bag of food for him. Grisca came out of his room, mewing happily. Unlike Isabel, she never seemed to worry overmuch that Willem's return was temporary. She just enjoyed having her boy back.

There were times Isabel wished she were more like her cat.

Willem bounded out of his room, laughing as Grisca chased him to the stables. Isabel heard Tremaud whinny—a happy, triumphant sound. The stallion always welcomed Willem's return with joy.

Stepping out of the cottage, she watched as Willem saddled the horse. His sword gleamed in the sun, the steel shining almost as brightly as the clear stone at the pommel that seemed to split the sunlight into a thousand colours as he swung himself into the saddle. Tremaud reared, and Willem laughed.

Smiling, Isabel walked out toward them and handed him the sack of food, then passed him a waterskin.

"Thank you." His smile was tender. Her beloved son.

"Go do good, Willem."

"Always, mother." He turned Tremaud and thundered off down the path.

"You have fours weeks, my son. Use them wisely." Isabel sighed and looked down at Grisca.

The cat rubbed against her. Isabel bent down and picked her up, moaning as her back twinged in sudden pain. Cradling Grisca to her chest, she closed her eyes tightly. Why did each goodbye hurt more?

She sniffed but refused to cry. The wizard had changed her destiny, too, when he'd cursed her son. She'd accepted that. What she hadn't been able to accept was that Willem would be all alone when she died. She'd tried taking on an apprentice—someone who could learn the ancient arts from her, who could take her place someday and give Willem these small chances at life. The first girl had run off with the miller's boy before the moon had cycled twice. The next girl had made it longer, had even shown promise—until a fever had taken her. The third girl had been waylaid on the road— she'd managed to escape but had run back to her village, deciding to stay where it was safe.

Isabel had given up after that. She'd said prayers and worked magic, asking, beseeching, willing the forces that drove the sun and the moon to send her someone to take her place and take care of her son. She'd imagined she felt something each time she prayed, and often thought she heard a voice like the wind through the trees saying, "It shall be done." But it hadn't been done. And she was running out of time.

She'd tried enchanting herself as a last resort, knowing how dangerous it might prove to be, but she'd been out of options and willing to take the risk. Once she was gone, her boy was destined to lie silently on his bed, never coming to life, even for these brief moments. It had taken a lot of studying—and a few bribes in coin or trade—to find out the details of the spell. Like much magic, it was relatively simple, one only needed the will behind it. And she'd had plenty of that. But the spell failed; she kept aging. She gave up then. Gave up trying, and gave up believing that help might come—except for those rare occasions when she heard the wind through the trees and thought it sounded like it was saying, "Soon."

Grisca licked her cheek, then wriggled out of her arms, landing gracefully and running back into the house. Isabel followed, going into Willem's room and changing the linens. They might not ever turn stale because of her spells, but she wanted him to return to new sheets. It was one of the few things she could do for him...other than giving him the forfeited destinies. Opening the window, she let fresh air come in. She and Grisca would strengthen the spell later. For now, they would let the air move freely, as Willem did.

She heard a noise in the main room and followed the sound. Grisca had knocked the candle over; the flame had gone out but dark crimson wax spilled gently onto the table. The cat pawed through the cards until she knocked two free of the deck. She looked up at Isabel expectantly.

Sighing, Isabel went into her stillroom and took a small wax figure from a carved box. She carried it out to the hearth and carefully cut the red thread that surrounded the figure, unwinding it slowly to keep it from breaking. When the thread turned black in four short weeks, Willem would return to her.

She studied the wax figure, touching it gently—Leopold, with his new destiny. She stood and walked to the garden, stopping at the root cellar to pull out a small bulb. Kneeling next to the bed of striplings, she dug a small hole and buried the wax figure underneath the bulb, then covered them both up and watered the area well.

One of the plants that had been dying yesterday lay flat on the ground, its leaves withered and black. Martin had died. A hunting accident. She'd seen it in the cards after he'd left to find a new, more idle life, and Willem had ridden off with his destiny. She knew how all of their destinies would go—these retiring champions—and she hated that she knew.

Grisca came out, holding the two cards in her mouth, face down. Isabel held out her hand, and the cat dropped the cards in her palm.

Isabel stared at them. Leopold's new destiny. The moment she turned them over, she would know all. She shoved them into the pocket of her skirt.

Grisca meowed, sounding both impatient and confused.

"Let's not look this time." Pushing herself up, Isabel walked back into the house and buried the cards in the deck, shuffling repeatedly to clear them of Leopold's destiny.

Grisca watched her, one paw on the table. She mewed again, the question apparent: "Why?"

"I'd rather not know. I want to believe Leopold will be happy. That he'll grow old and live to see his grandchildren have babies of their own."

Until she looked, it was as likely as any other future. At any rate, she'd only have to watch his plant to know how he fared.

She took a deep breath. "Would you like to go down to the sea, Grisca?" It would be better than simply sitting in the house waiting for Willem to come home. And it had been ages since she'd sat out at night listening to the waves crash against the rocks.

Grisca meowed, an approving sound, and as Isabel picked her up, she thought she heard a sound like the wind through the trees. Closing her eyes, she waited for some sign, some word. But there was nothing. Just as there was nothing left for her to do but wait for her son to come home. She sighed and felt the breath wheeze in her chest. The magic was draining her now; she'd always known it would come to this—she'd just wanted a different destiny for herself, too.

The sea would be different, if only for a few days. Putting the cat down, she said, "We'll see if Mister Waring will let us borrow his cart."

She began to pack. Once again ignoring the room down the hall. The room that for now was empty of life. And blessedly empty of responsibility—of burden.

Her Willem. No mother had ever loved a son more.

*

Isabel watered the striplings, smiling as she saw how much Leopold's plant had grown since she'd planted it. He and Marthe obviously prospered, and he seemed to have inherited a farmer's destiny. Marthe's formerly neglected lands now sprouted new life everywhere, and her once-thin animals were fat and glossy with good health. Marthe too looked happy and healthy, and a bit fatter herself—in the belly, where Isabel liked to think that the first of the children Leopold had so desired perhaps grew.

It was hard to believe that Leopold had only arrived six weeks ago, he seemed so much a part of the village already—and of Isabel's life. He'd stopped by to check on her quite often, laughing whenever Grisca ran out to meet him.

Isabel looked for the cat and saw her sitting on the fence near Tremaud. She seemed to be staring down the road, as she often did when Willem was due back from his respites from lifelessness. Only Willem had returned two weeks ago, struck down in Leopold's place as Isabel had known he would be.

It had been a struggle to get him back to his bed this time. Her magic had not worked as well as it had in the past when she'd tried to use it to make her son lighter. She knew that it would only get more difficult as her magic began to really fail her.

She closed her eyes, opening herself up to the earth, the sky, the power that pulsed through all of life. "Please," she said, her words barely more than a breath. "Please don't leave my son alone."

Tremaud nickered, his mane blowing as a breeze came up, rustling the trees. The wind seemed to mock her, as her word echoed back: "Alo-o-o-o-o-ne."

Hoof beats sounded on the road, and Isabel sighed. She was in no mood to help any of the villagers today, didn't feel as if she had enough power to do the easiest working. She saw Grisca stand up and stretch, then leap down and take off running for the road, as if to meet the coming rider.

Tremaud whinnied—a loud, challenging sound.

Another horse answered, then came into sight with her red mane flying and her tail held high as she slid to a stop.

Grisca was running behind her and leapt to the horse's back, then onto the shoulder of her rider, who laughed.

"Your cat is crazy, Isabel." Leopold's voice held amusement, and he put his face close to Grisca's, not objecting when she licked him.

Casha danced underneath him, whinnying to Tremaud, who was prancing in his corral.

"You offered me his services once?" Leopold patted Casha's neck. "My mare is in heat, and I thought..."

Isabel laughed softly. She wasn't sure if the stallion was still fertile—the spell that prolonged his life might not have sustained his virility. But it wouldn't hurt to try. Certainly the stallion seemed ready, so she motioned for Leopold to proceed.

He unsaddled Casha and let her loose in the paddock. They watched as nature took its exuberant course, then left the horses alone and went into the house.

"You're well, Isabel?" Leopold asked as he moved almost restlessly around her front room.

"I am." She sat down wearily. "Old, but well. And you? I hear good things of your livestock and produce."

He smiled. "The farm thrives." Then his smile faded a bit. "Marthe credits our good fortune to my expertise."

"Is she wrong?" A farmer's destiny was certainly not unlikely.

He was silent as he stood at her hearth, fingering what was left of the crimson candle she'd burned when she took his original destiny from him.

"Is something wrong, Leopold?"

He turned to her, and there was such torment in his gaze that she gasped and held her hand out.

"Leopold, what is it?"

He shook his head, his eyes darting away, as if meeting her gaze would reveal too much.

"Leopold?"

Grisca came in and rubbed against his legs. He picked her up, cradling her against his chin, and she seemed to go limp. Many moments passed, the little house silent except for the sound of the cat's purring.

Finally, he looked over at her. "Something's wrong. I don't think I am a farmer."

She frowned.

"The memory gaps I have...I believe I know what they should be." He began to pace, still holding the cat. "I believe I'm missing knowledge...things I should know."

Her frown grew deeper. None of her former champions had ever said such a thing. Had she made a mistake with the herbs? Or had her magic not been up to the task this time?

He moved to her, staring down at her. "I do nothing to my plants to make them grow except wish that they do so...and they thrive. I think how our flocks and herds should look, and they grow healthy and fat. And there are other things..."

"What other things?"

Grisca leapt out of his arms and jumped to the table. She lay down by the cards, her paws folded under her chest.

"I know things. Things I shouldn't know." He turned, walking into the hall, and Isabel rose and followed him.

He stopped in front of Willem's room and turned to look at her. "This is your son's room."

She nodded, then the hackles on the back of her neck rose as he moved his hand over the door, easily dismantling the spell she and Grisca had put there. The wind whipped up outside; she could hear it whistling through the trees as Leopold opened the door and walked into Willem's room.

"Isabel, I've seen him in my dreams. He...he calls to me." Leopold turned to her. "You call to me also." He swallowed hard, as if he could barely take in what he was saying. "I know things. Words that make water cold on a hot day or make an apple ripen as I hold it. I can feel the moon move across the sky. I can see futures when I look deep into someone's eyes." He brushed past her, hurrying out to where Grisca still sat by the cards.

The cat rose; she batted at the deck, knocking the cards, two of them falling to the ground to land face down. Moving again, she hit two more cards, and they landed on top of the first two. Leopold reached down and pulled out the bottom two cards, turning them over slowly.

Death. And the Ten of Swords.

"I see these in my dreams too, Isabel. Always behind me."

Isabel could see the pain in his face as he stared at the cards. He remembered too much for her to try to lie to him. Or at least lie completely. She could give him a cleaned-up version of the truth. "They were once your destiny, but you changed that."

"No, you changed that. I shouldn't know that, should I? And yet I do." He touched the cards. "These signify a violent death. I can read them. I shouldn't be able to do that, either."

He picked the other two cards up, handing them to her without looking at them. She could feel the cards pulsing in her hands and slowly turned them over.

The Magician and Judgment.

"I hear your voice, Isabel, crying out to heaven. In my dreams, I hear you, and I see these cards. And I know what I must do." He knelt in front of her. "I must help you. I must learn from you. I am... needed. Still needed."

He reached out and found Grisca without ever taking his eyes off of Isabel. He stroked the cat, and she purred again, even louder.

"I know all this," he said, "and yet, I don't understand how or why I know it."

Isabel stared down at the cards. She'd asked for this. She needed this. But not him. Not this good man who'd only wanted a life of his own. "I can't ask this of you, Leopold. You don't deserve this fate."

He smiled gently. "Neither does that young man lying in there. Your son, your heart—would you rather he was left here all alone?"

She looked down at his cards, then at those on the floor. Death—that would be her card soon. There was just enough time to train him, to teach him.

To trap him.

She stood up, reaching down for his old destiny, pulling the cards up to join the two she held. She reached for the rest of the deck and had to push Grisca away to get them all.

"I release you. I release you. I release you," she said as she shuffled the cards.

"Isabel." His voice was full of infinite patience...and amusement. As if he already understood destiny better than she.

Grisca batted at Isabel in a way that was not quite playful. Ignoring the cat, she cut the cards and fanned them out.

"Pick two now."

He did and turned them over.

Judgment. And the Magician.

He didn't look surprised as he took her hands. "Teach me, Isabel? Teach me what I need to know?"

Grisca rubbed against her hand, licking her softly.

"It's my destiny, isn't it?" He smiled at her, a sad smile, as if somewhere deep inside himself he understood the price of his words.

She shook her head—a stubborn old woman to the end. "It's my destiny." She looked at him, at his handsome face. So earnest, so willing.

Turning away from him, she walked into Willem's room and stared down at her son, tracing his warm, ever-young cheek.

"Tell me why I see him," Leopold said from behind her. She hadn't heard him follow her in. "Tell me what happened to him."

His hand settled on her shoulder, warm and human—he was possibly the first human to touch her in a long time. Other than Willem, if he remembered to hug her before he charged off to meet someone else's fate.

"I release you," she whispered, knowing the words meant nothing to anyone but her and this fine young man who was offering to take her place.

"Tell me how I can help." His hand tightened on her shoulder and she could feel his life force surging, strong and ready to do whatever was necessary. A willing apprentice.

And more a son than Willem seemed these days. She closed her eyes, blinking back tears. Lifting her hand, she let it rest on top of his and sensed her own life force rising to meet his. She felt a surge of energy as if her power were growing as it merged with his in a way she'd never known before.

Magic calling to magic.

The wind whipped up, suddenly surging through the trees, blowing the front door shut. She heard Tremaud and Casha neighing in the corral. Grisca ran in from the other room and jumped onto the bed, curling next to Willem and closing her eyes.

"Tell me," Leopold said. "Tell me everything."

She shook her head, but her mouth wouldn't obey her heart. It was as if a dam had broken deep inside her, and words came flooding out of her.

She told him everything, and as she spoke, the wind died down—a promise finally kept.

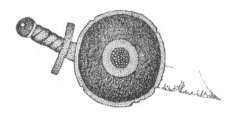

THE CITY OF SILENCE

Eric Ian Steele

The Once-King rode out of the West on the back of the storm. His muscled wrists pulled tight on the reins of his lumbering steed, a giant warhorse bedecked with chainmail. Behind him, the one-eyed seer Obadiah, lurched to a halt, shaken from his innermost reveries by the sudden stop of his mighty liege. The former king had not spoken since leaving their kingdom, though the ride had taken many days. During that time King Ariston said nought but glared into the fire when they made camp until long after the embers had turned to ashes.

Before them lay a castellated city, its lofty walls cut from white stone. A stone pyramid dominated the skyline, surrounded by slender minarets. Yet, as Obadiah strained his eye to see the inhabitants of this unknown place, he found no evidence of life, no bustle in the marketplace that he glimpsed through the winding streets, no beasts of burden traipsing through the iron gates that stayed severely shut against the outside world. No bells tolled from the temples, no prayers rang out from the minarets. The place lay as silent as the bottom of the ocean. As silent as his king had been these past six weeks, Obadiah thought with little satisfaction.

King Ariston gave his advisor a curious glance. Beneath the heavy brows, dark eyes glittered with a fire that had extinguished the lives of many. A fire that had brought them here. He wished he could convince his master to turn back, to once again rule the loving kingdom that was their own. But all his words of kindness and his learned philosophies had failed to dent the king's resolve. Whatever battle his master was facing, Obadiah knew, he must win it alone.

"I recognize this place from the maps in the palace libraries," the old seer said. The thought of those towering rooms filled with musk-scented volumes of lore - a place he had loved until recently - filled him with aching loss. "This is the City of Dreams, Lost Jabur. The sultan is said to have the richest court in this part of the world. He surrounds himself with minstrels and troubadours, while his harem comprises the loveliest dancing girls in all the Eastern realms."

Ariston gave a grunt, his jaw jutting out like the edge of a granite cliff. Evidently, he was unimpressed. Obadiah knew that the best jesters and minstrels in the land had failed to cheer his master. Little wonder, then, that he scorned such pleasure now.

"Of course, your highness cares little for these things," he said. "Yet our horses may grow weary even if we do not. It may be prudent to go down there and feed and water them, if we expect them to carry us much further."

The king considered. His lip furled in amusement. The old vizier blushed, for he too wished to be fed and watered, preferably in a comfortable inn.

"Forgive me, sire," he said. "My old bones can only stand so much of this desert floor before they begin to ache for a silken bed."

The king's gaze darted away, admonished by the aged vizier. He darkened once more and nodded. The two of them steered their horses toward the white city that stood like a fancifully-carved jewellery box against the desolation of the lone and level sands. Not a tree nor bush grew on the plain of Jabur. The city had been called a paradise by scholars. Its many fragrant gardens were the product of careful cultivation from a series of underground wells. Only the nearby gnawing of a solitary vulture upon a desert snake disturbed the dumb quietude of the plain.

They reached the mammoth iron gates. Letters four feet high carved upon them read; "THOU SHALT NOT SIN".

The king halted once more and cast a questing glance at his vizier, but Obadiah knew not what those words might portend. In response, Ariston rode up to the iron gates and rapped his huge knuckles upon the metal, producing a cold, hard echo.

Slowly, the gates creaked open. Within, the city lay in silence. No street urchins played in dusty roads, no creaking carts wound their way to market, no goodwife fluttered her washing from the windows of the shuttered houses. No guard manned the gate. The entire gatehouse seemed to operate on a system of great chains and pulleys. But who operated those chains? Ariston whirled around his horse, expecting a flurry of arrows from some hidden quarter, but none came.

"Curious," said the vizier. "I wonder where those chains lead, and who pulls the pulleys?"

Ariston waited for a moment, his muscles bunched in readiness beneath his leather tunic, the sole remnants of his former finery. His head lay bare, devoid of the jewel-encrusted crown that once adorned it. The journey had tanned his skin to a leathery hide, bronzed by the noonday sun. Woe betide any who should fall upon the cutting edge of his sword, the vizier thought. Satisfied they were not under attack, he advanced into the city at a pace slow enough for the vizier to reluctantly follow on his own dust-caked nag.

They saw no soul living nor dead until they came to an inn. The stone structure seemed well-cared for, though devoid of the usual sounds of laughter and pleasure. Indeed, the place was handsomely decorated with many piping fauns in the stonework. Polished wooden doors beckoned. The King waited for the vizier to join him, then pushed his way inside.

Within, a dark wooden bar, polished wooden floors and walls covered in fine tapestries greeted them. All might be well here save for the absence of mirth. A young woman, plain of dress, flaxen-haired and sullen-eyed, observed them from behind the bar. An older man emerged from the back room, well-fed but similarly clad in a plain cotton tunic and pants. He bustled the girl into the back room with a scowl of disapproval, then plastered on a smile and came wallowing toward them.

"Welcome, friends. Please, be seated," he said. "May I bring you water?"

"I prefer wine but I believe my lord will take ale," said the vizier.

"Alas, we do not serve such beverages here," the man said. "There has been no wine in the city for many a year. All I can offer is water or lotus flower."

Obadiah grew nervous upon seeing the mild irritation in his liege's eye. He spoke up. "No wine, no beer? What manner of alehouse is this?"

"Pardon, sirs," said the innkeeper, stroking the long waxed beard which men of that region cultivated. "But our laws forbid the consumption of such substances. It increases the already sanguine temperament of men. We are all genteel here, now. Come, please sample one of my blue lotus blossoms, guaranteed to dull the appetite and lull the mind into a most pleasant state of stupefaction."

"But do your people not believe alcohol is a gift from the gods to grant us happiness?" said the vizier.

The innkeeper grew uncomfortable. "Forgive me, sirs. But I know little of such things. I am just an innkeeper." And he withdrew again.

"Well, what a strange kind of tavern this is," said Obadiah. "No wine, only water. No wonder the place is quiet. What life is it for men who labour without the refreshment of the gods?"

King Ariston said nothing. The innkeeper returned and placed a copper jug of water before them. He drank, and stared into the cold grate of the unlit fireplace. But if he looked for the answers to life's questions there, he found nothing.

The sounds of footsteps drew close, and with them they heard the unmistakable chink of armour. The doors opened, and half a dozen soldiers in studded leather armour and sun-tarnished helmets entered. Each one had a shaven head with a single red triangle painted upon it. At the front of this phalanx stood a haughty official, clad in the same armour but without the curved swords of the others. He wore his hair in the short, oil-curled style of the city-dwellers whom they had left behind.

"I see you have guests, innkeeper," said the man in educated tones. His voice sounded high as a girl's, yet his profile spoke of an aquiline cruelty. He turned to the visitors. Obadiah nursed his cup, casting a nervous glance at his liege. "I am Afrodicius, counsellor to the Queen Jaramsheela the Merciful. May I join you?" the man asked. He sat down anyway. The guards shifted by the entrance.

"Then the prosperous Sultan of Jabur is no more?" Obadiah asked. "I read that his mighty sway extended across the entire plain."

"The sultan is gone," said the man, wiping his lips with derision. "His wife, Queen Jaramsheela, rules in his place. It has been thus the past twenty years."

"And is it still favourable to travellers?" asked the vizier. "I read that the Sultan extended his hospitality to all who desired it."

"Our queen welcomes all who abide by our laws," said Afrodicius. "Provided they swear obeisance to her and give her what is theirs, for in this land no man may profit from his own labour. All is given to the kingdom, that it may be used for the public good."

Obadiah saw that this man was eyeing Ariston's jewel-encrusted scabbard.

"I think I see," said Obadiah. "And what of those who do not agree?"

Ariston's massive thews bunched as he gripped the cup, the tendons in his neck taut with readiness. Obadiah knew well that his king did not trust this high-voiced, slithering serpent of a man whose eyes never blinked nor held any semblance of a soul.

"There are none," Afrodicius said. "Not anymore."

Where other men might have spoken at length, Ariston acted. His swiftness took the others by surprise. As his eyes had read treachery in the sudden stiffness of his opponent's body, so his fingers grasped the hilt of his sword without betraying his own thoughts. Schooled by many battles, his blade scythed out of its scabbard, propelled by the iron-muscled arm of its owner. The keen edge sliced clean through the leather jerkin of the first man who approached, tearing fibre and flesh, disembowelling him before Ariston had even stood to his feet.

The thin, swarthy leader of the guards leapt back out of killing range. Ariston swung his sword in a wide arc, severing the trachea of the second guard who had approached. The guard crumbled to his knees, bubbling blood from his astonished lips.

The King grinned through teeth like tombstones as his blade roared through the room, singing with a shrill song as it hacked a third man to pieces, severing an arm with one sweep and a leg with the other. Screams filled the tavern and blood decorated the grease-spotted walls. King Ariston was moving now with the grace of a panther, his sword slicing almost faster than the eye could follow. A fourth man met his death at the hands of that greedy blade. Still it sang, hungry for more souls.

But no man can fend off an army single-handed. At length more guards appeared and overpowered him by force of numbers alone, gripping his weapon arm and shoulders and pulling him to the ground by his legs. Afrodicius kept his distance and endangered his person not, but more and more guards threw themselves upon the mighty king until they smothered him like a blanket snuffing out a mighty flame. A club descended upon the back of King Ariston's head, and he slumped forward onto the ground like some drink-addled sot. The battle was done.

Obadiah gasped. A moment later, sword points thrust at his throat. Afrodicius checked the unconscious foe. Satisfied, he turned to the old man.

"You too in time will learn to call my mistress Queen," he said.

Obadiah grew stubborn. Once too often he had seen his king brought low. "I no longer care for this world," he said. "My loyalty is to my king alone - Ariston the Mighty, ruler of Hylo, Emperor of the Westernewake, he who has crushed armies with his bare hands, and who lives unchallenged by all who live by the western seas."

"There are no seas here. And there are no lands but ours," said Afrodicius, untroubled. "To talk otherwise is heresy. You will find a great many things are heresy. Yet there is only one punishment. We find that it is most effective."

"We broke no law," said Obadiah.

"You have failed to submit to the queen upon your arrival. Silence is not an option. Yet perhaps she will take pity upon you, seeing as you are strangers here. Heed my advice, old man, and bind your tongue, lest it be bound for you."

He gestured to the soldiers who dragged the fallen monarch outside. It took four of them to carry his massive body. Obadiah considered his options, then followed.

The soldiers traversed the city toward the massive stone pyramid at its centre. More guards adorned its tiers, all voiceless. The bronze doors at its base opened, and Afrodicius led them into blackness beyond. Obadiah's eyes adjusted to the darkness after several minutes, allowing him to make out the green stone passageways that riddled the monolith. After an age of wandering the meandering tunnels, they came to the throne room of Jaramsheela herself.

The queen reclined upon a couch of rare and exotic furs, her milk-white body clad in an enticing satin kirtle that disguised very little of her obvious charms. A woman still in her youth, her eyes glittered like opals beneath her mantle of coal-black hair. She rose upon seeing the body of Ariston dragged before her and dumped on the dusty floor in an uneven heap.

"What is this? Is it a man?" she asked.

"Intruders, ma'am," Afrodicius said, on bended knee. "The old one says he follows a western king named Ariston.

This other we rendered helpless, but not before he slew many of us."

"Indeed. Then perhaps you are not the leader of guards that I thought you were," the queen said. Afrodicius looked uncomfortable. "And who is this king?"

A vicious hand shoved Obadiah to his knees.

"Your highness," the old vizier spoke. "Forgive us, please. We knew not who rules this place, or we would have paid our due respects. We are but travellers, many days from our home. We seek only shelter and rest before we resume our journey."

He watched the queen stalk toward them. He saw the look on her face as she appreciated King Ariston's size and strength. "I think not," she said. "We need workers such as this. And even a one-eyed old man may be useful. Bind them both, put chains on the big one, and gave him water."

They did thus, snapping a chain collar around Ariston's muscular neck, manacles about his wrists and ankles. The old man they bound with rope. The captain of the guard splashed water on Ariston's face, then poured some down his throat. The King spluttered and woke. Then his eyes fell upon the queen, and he grew silent.

"I see you watch me with sullen eyes," she said. "Sullen, traitorous eyes. You wish I was dead, do you not?"

"Nay, majesty," said Obadiah. A sharp blow from a sword pommel sent him sprawling.

"I could easily command your respect, old man, if I tore out your tongue by the root, just as I have done to all others who oppose me." Hey eyes lighted upon Ariston. "But you are not my concern. This one here, he glares at me like an insolent dog. I could never command the respect of him. He will work for me, but not in his present condition. He must be subdued by other means. Humiliation first, then bondage."

"Geld him, my lady?" said Afrodicius, with all too-obvious enthusiasm.

"No, Afrodicius," she said. "A more appropriate penalty for a swordsman. Something that will make him remember that he will never be what he once was. He will always be a slave."

Ariston's emerald eyes burned with such fire that it made Obadiah's tremble.

"I should have your tongue torn out, but I doubt it would serve any use. No, for you speech is unimportant. We must first break the spirit before we conquer the mind." She pointed to a guard with a huge, curved scimitar. "Cut off his hand. The right one. I see his scabbard is on his left. That way he will never raise a weapon against me or any other."

"No, your highness!" Obadiah cried.

Afrodicius grabbed the man by the neck and hauled him to his feet. "Nobody says "no" to the queen," he said.

"Leave him be," said the queen. Afrodicius retreated, stung. The queen enjoyed the discomfort of her lieutenant. She licked her lips, as if savouring the taste of power. "He is old. Nobody will listen to an old man. But this one... this one will provide a worthy lesson to any who wish to defy our rule."

The guards grabbed Ariston's sinuous frame. He attempted to resist but another blow to his head robbed him of most of his senses. Another guard's fist pummelled him in the base of the spine, and he collapsed forward, straining not to kiss the earth once more.

"Hold him," said Afrodicius. The others stretched out Ariston's right wrist. The king's fingers clawed for release - if but one of them had managed to reach a sword the struggle would have been over. But no blade lay close by. A massive guard raised his two-handed scimitar and brought the blade down smartly on Ariston's wrist. The steel chopped through blood and bone, muscle and tissue. The hand that had once belonged to a king now belonged to nothing. One of the guards held it up to show his queen. Then he threw it away.

Ariston sagged to the floor, gasping. No scream escaped his lips, yet he looked pale and weak. Obadiah withdrew his eyes from the dreadful sight.

"Bind him," said the queen. "Make sure he lives. If he dies all your heads will be forfeit."

She sat back down on her throne, her lips quivering in a vulpine smile. "I want him to survive a long time."

The soldiers hurried to fetch the court healers. Obadiah watched while they cauterized the bloodied stump. This time Ariston did scream in a bellow that echoed throughout the corridors of green stone, a horrible sound fit enough to kill birds in flight or bring the dead up out of the ground. The healers stitched the wound, placed the stump in a leather cup and bandaged it to his chest.

After several hours, the two were let go, out into the street, the guards kicking them into the dirt for good measure.

A dust storm had risen up. They staggered through the wind-swept, silent streets. Obadiah supported his king's hulking body as best he could. Sometimes he swore he saw lithe forms at windows or hiding behind shutters looking out. But none offered help. The wind laughed at them. And he wondered how he would survive on these streets. Would he and his lord become beggars, unable to work? There seemed no need for learned men in a place such as this.

Then a door clapped shut, and a thin figure darted through the dust-storm toward them. A girl, wearing a simple woollen kirtle, a scarf wrapped around her face to protect her from the dust. He recognized her –the girl from the inn.

"Are you all right?" she asked. Then she saw Ariston's bandaged stump and gasped. "Come, back to my father's. We will see what can be done."

*

Over the next few weeks the vizier watched his king writhe upon the threadbare sofa in the inn, battling a fever. He soon learned the girl's name was Mira. She and her father, Osiris, agreed to rent them the spare room in the tavern next to the cramped compartments where she and her father resided. The innkeeper was none too happy with this arrangement, but gave in to the concerted imploring of his daughter on one proviso – that as soon as the warrior could walk he would leave their company. No-one liked a pariah, and his injury marked him as one who had offended the queen.

"As soon as he is mended you must leave the city," he said.

"But where will we go?" Obadiah asked. "How will we fend for ourselves in the desert without my lord's sword?"

"That is your affair," said the innkeeper. "You should have thought of that before you offended her highness. We have to live here, and I will not have my daughter placed in one of Afrodicus's harem pits on account of someone we hardly know."

Obadiah said nothing. He could well understand the man's concern for his daughter. He took the fresh water bowl from Mira with gratitude and wiped his master's sweat-beaded brow. The once-king's dreadful fever threatened to consume him. In the days that followed it grew worse. Ariston mumbled in his delirium. Once he reached out and grabbed Obadiah by the throat and almost shook the life out of him before the old man could escape the iron grip.

Obadiah ministered to the fallen warrior with herbs Mira bought for him. She did not appear to recognize the medicinal properties of these plants, although they were common enough.

"How do you know these things? Is it sorcery?" she asked.

"You have no schooling in medicine?" Obadiah asked. Mira shook her head. "Well, it is not sorcery. Some plants can soothe a fever. Afterwards, I can drain the body of sickness, like so." He sliced open a fresh wound on Ariston's chest and bled it into a cup. "In Hylo even children are taught how to heal. What do they teach here?"

"They teach how to worship Jaramsheela, our queen, and how to dance for the pleasure of my lord Afrodicius. All other learning is forbidden."

"How did it come to be thus?" asked the vizier.

Mira took the cup from him and emptied it out into a bowl. She handed the vizier a fresh jug of water, into which he dipped a new poultice of herbs. "When the old Sultan died, his queen took his place. It is said she comes from the swamp-drenched jungles of Tirzah. As soon as she ascended, she passed laws commanding we obey her. Those who did not agree were either killed by Afrodicius and his men or silenced by having their tongues torn out by the roots. That is why the city is so quiet."

"Did no-one rise up against her?" Obadiah asked, startled.

"Some did. But most were too cowardly and afraid to fight. They said Jaramsheela's laws did not seem unreasonable. But then she passed more and more laws, until she and Afrodicius ruled alone and all the viziers were expelled or cut down. It became treason to speak ill of anything. She mutilated all who spoke out."

"Then this is a city of silence," said Obadiah. He laid the poultice on the king's forehead. Ariston moaned in reply. The sickness ran deep, and Obadiah wondered if he too was on the verge of being silenced forever.

The seventh day of fever came and went, then the eighth. Mira came in to check on them and saw Obadiah praying to Urthona for guidance.

"What are you doing?" she asked.

"I am asking the great god Urthona, the god of scholars and prophecy, for aid," he said. "Do your people not pray to any gods?"

"We may have no gods. The queen forbade it. She calls it heresy. She says that religion is but a tool to control the people."

"There is some truth to that," Obadiah said with a rueful smirk. "But it is not all truth. We human beings have much power, yet we are but ants compared to the wonders of the universe. How then can we presume to know all that exists?

Mira considered. "You are a wise man."

"My only wisdom consists in knowing that I do not know all."

A smile came to the woman's lips.

"Ah, see?" Obadiah said. "If one may still smile amid such desolation there may yet be hope for mankind."

Ariston groaned in his bed. His fingers clenched around the bedpost, and his knuckles grew white, until Obadiah thought he might snap the post clean off. Then he relaxed again and slept.

"What does he speak of?" Mira said. "He keeps saying

one word over and over: 'Quantok.' What does it mean?"

Obadiah rose and wandered to the window. He looked out over the deserted city. The only fires blazed atop the distant pyramid.

"Quantok was his brother," said the vizier. "He had eleven of them. Sons of Har and Heva, first king and queen of the Westernewake. Ariston was eldest, and so the throne passed to him after Old Har died. But the brothers grew jealous and fought over the land. Many died. There were long wars, so bitter that brother fought brother, fathers disowned sons, and sons slew their fathers. At length, the sons of Har agreed that they should cease hostilities and each possess a portion of the entire kingdom. Yet Quantok thought his share should have been larger, and so he fought on. One night, he raided Ariston's palace with a band of assassins. He would have slain my master in bed but for my lord's wife, Queen Camelia. She threw herself in front of her brother-in-law's blade and died. On seeing this, Ariston wrenched Quantok's sword out of his grip and beheaded his brother where he stood."

Mira said nothing. Obadiah supposed she understood well how madness could seize the most rational heart in times of trouble.

"After that, my lord spoke no more. He gave up his mantle of kingship and passed it to his brother, Hylo. He left the land on horseback that night, destined for who knew where. I saw him and caught up to him, and we have been travelling together ever since. Yet he has not spoken a word except sometimes the names of his brother and wife in his sleep."

"He must be deeply troubled," Mira said.

"My lord is a great warrior, but he knows only how to kill," said the vizier. "Peace does not sit well upon his shoulders."

He looked at the fallen king, with his sweat-drenched locks tossing amid his fever-dream, and hoped Urthona would not require too great a sacrifice.

*

After ten days Afrodicius and his guards came once more. By this time, the fever had broken. The old king still lay weak and grey from his ordeal. The queen's captain frowned down upon the sick man with a disdainful sneer.

"Send him to work when he is ready," he said. "Have him pull carts or, better yet, work the mines. Something where he can learn humility and his place in society."

He turned to Obadiah with a contemptuous smirk. "As for his vizier, put him to work transcribing the speeches of our queen. Know, old man, that the only writings allowed in Jabur are those sanctioned by the queen herself. You will help copy them so that every household will know the queen's wisdom."

He sensed the old vizier's reluctance. "Or perhaps you wish to join your master in our salt mines, or acting as a beast of burden?"

"I will do as you ask," said Obadiah, his head bowed in submission.

Afrodicius retreated, apparently disappointed that the old man offered no resistance this time.

"You must be careful," said Mira, when they had gone. "No-one lives to defy the queen a second time. You are lucky your king did not have his tongue torn out by the roots. That is what happened to my brother."

"You have a brother?" Obadiah asked.

"He is a blacksmith on the other side of the city. He made the mistake of questioning Afrodicius in an open marketplace."

"Tell me more of this Queen of yours," Obadiah said.

"There is not much to tell. She has been queen ever since I can remember. They say she keeps herself young through sorcery, and that she holds men's hearts through the same witchcraft. Those she cannot enslave she silences like my brother. "

Obadiah watched Ariston writhe in a sudden spasm of pain. Though the danger was passed, the stump of a wrist looked bruised and painful. Yet Obadiah no longer despaired. He had formulated a plan. "Take me to your brother," he said. "I presume they still have precious gems in this city?"

"It is what Jabur was once famous for. We have some of the largest gemstone mines in the kingdom. Their wealth allowed Afrodicius to raise a great army of mercenaries when she took over and destroyed any resistance from the other caliphs. Why?"

Obadiah smiled in return. "I will teach you something of magi. If Urthona is willing, perhaps we can turn Jaramsheela's own resources against her."

He ignored the girl's confused stare but bid her hurry. Out the window, he watched her race across the street. No sound came from the city. The buildings remained dark within, tomb-like and desolate. A few silent labourers carried large earthen jars on their heads through the wind-swept streets. Only the sands spoke, the wind whistling across the flat roofs. Obadiah turned back to the semi-conscious body on the sofa.

"I think you shall be avenged soon enough, my king."

Mira brought her brother, Shem. The man was a strong youth with a short clipped beard. His skin bore the marks of rough treatment, scalds and burns from his smelting pit. Mira explained that although he could not talk, he could listen as well as any man. Obadiah sat him down and showed him on parchment what he had in mind. Shem looked confused at first, then mystified, then astonished, and finally nodded his assent.

"How long will it take?" Obadiah asked.

Shem held up ten fingers and pointed at the sun.

"Good," he said. "I think we had best begin. I want it done before my lord returns to health."

Shem went away. In the days that followed, they had ever-more frequent visits from the guards. Ariston's strength returned faster with each day. Yet Obadiah bid him pretend he was still weak from the torture. Each time the guards left him with a warning that they would return and that soon he would have to get up and work, the lazy dog.

After ten days, Shem returned, He held a bundle in his hands. He laid it down on the table and unwrapped it. "What is it?" Mira asked. "It looks like a – "

"A hand," said Obadiah, lifting up the block of green jade. "My lord," he said to the king. "Look what Shem has made for you?"

The king opened his eyes and sat upright. He stared at the green sculpture. His eyes filled with questions. "Fear not, my lord," said Obadiah. "I have yet to breathe life into these fingers."

Then he went away and performed his secret rites. He offered sacred things to Urthona. What these were no man may say. The truth is sometimes better left unsaid, and is unpalatable to many. Urthona can be a cruel god, though he always fulfils his promises. Yet he demands all a man can give – his life, his family, even his soul. Perhaps, given his history, Obadiah did promise more than he had the right to give. But that is another story

Many copper braziers burned with the remains of

livestock proffered by Mira that day, much to the protest of her father. But she won him over with the promise that this might be their salvation. The innkeeper had seen the mighty king in battle once, and he did not doubt that were he to be restored he might offer stout resistance to their overlords, so he assented. When he returned, Obadiah laid out the jade hand on the table and bid the once-king pick it up.

"Now, place it to your own wrist," he said.

The king did so, and at once a mighty pain wracked through him. He screamed in agony, a thing he had never done in all his many battles. His terrible cry, it is said, drowned out the temple bells and caused the palace guards to tremble and clutch at their spears.

When it was done, Ariston held up his wrist and flexed his new jade fingers.

"Sorcery," said Osiris the innkeeper.

"Indeed," Obadiah replied. "Sorcery to outwit a witch who has befuddled men's minds. You yourselves would have learned the old ways had not Jaramsheela forbade it, but in time perhaps I can teach one who is open to such knowledge."

He looked at Mira as he spoke, and she nodded.

King Ariston the Mighty rose. He stared at his fingers for a long time. Then he spoke with a voice as deep as a desert well. Obadiah and Shem sank to their knees.

"I am restored. My thanks to you, innkeeper, and your daughter, and to your son. And thanks to you, old friend. I had forgotten what a great seer you truly are."

"My only pleasure is to serve you, sire," said Obadiah.

"And my only wish is to fulfil your trust in me," said the king. "Though I can never return to my beloved lands, I see the faces of the oppressed here and it stirs my soul. Too long have I looked inwards to the black sea of my own thoughts.

Selfishness brought me here and the desire to escape my warlike past." He flexed his jade fingers. "But a man cannot escape his destiny. It follows him like a shadow. Stand, my friends. I am king no more, yet I may still be a warrior, as may you all. My vizier has already proven his worth. Now it is time for you to take the reins of your own futures. One man, no matter how mighty, cannot overcome an entire army. Yet I see in your face the fires of Orc. Rebellion blooms like a fiery flower in your bosoms." He looked at Shem. "Though your tongue is absent, you may still talk. A sharp sword speaks more eloquently than a thousand courtiers. Are there many more like you, weary of being held in silence?"

Shem nodded, his brows knitting with fierce determination.

"Then we have our army. I shall train you to use your weapons well. For unlike that haughty Afrodicius, we believe in our freedom. And a man who truly believes in his cause is worth ten who are forced to go along with a mad prophet for an easy life. Come, and I shall show you what is to be our training ground."

"But the guards," said Mira. "What shall I tell them?"

"Tell them I escaped," said King Ariston. "I will hide where no man will find me"

Ariston led Shem out into the dusty yard behind the inn, and began to teach him the basics of swordsmanship. To the blacksmith, the art was foreign. Since Jaramsheela's reign no man had ever been allowed to wield a sword except for the palace guards.

"My master is a great swordsman," Obadiah told Mira, as they watched the two men spar. "Have no fear. In time, your brother will lead an army that will put paid to those cravens in the pyramid yonder."

"I still fear for him," Mira said. "The queen has much powers of sorcery."

"Yes, you said," Obadiah said. "She lives a preternaturally long life. Yet she worships no god nor offers any prayers. Strange."

"Perhaps she does offer sacrifices. She has many maidens taken to the palace," Mira said. "No-one knows the reason why. None return."

The old man listened, troubled. He thought he knew the answer, yet he did not want to trouble the girl. If he was correct in his assumption, the King would have another problem to deal with.

*

After a week, Afrodicius came demanding to know the whereabouts of Ariston. The innkeeper told him as he had been instructed. The captain threatened and cajoled but when he could see that neither of them knew the answer, he let them go. As for Obadiah, they had forgotten about him in their madness. The guards rampaged through the city, searching houses and keeping a watch night and day on the walls. Little did Afrodicius know that Ariston lay not ten feet below his sandals, in the filthy crawlspace under the inn, sleeping with snakes and rats for company. These vermin disturbed not the king's slumber. Obadiah had given him ointments that would keep them away.

At night, they gathered together whoever would listen. Shem had friends who, while afraid to speak openly, sympathised with his plight. They met at the tavern while Ariston told them of his own kingdom, and how it was possible for a handful of men to triumph against many by guile and stealth. They devised their attack plans against those from the pyramid. It was a grand plan involving nets and ambush tactics. Obadiah gladdened as the Once-King again became the mighty leader he had been in his youth. Truly he was born to slaughter.

Then, on the second week, something unforeseen happened. Afrodicius and his guards dragged Mira away to the pyramid, promising that she would be released should Ariston give himself up 'ere nightfall.

"Tell me," Obadiah said to Osiris. "This queen of yours, does she ever leave the pyramid?"

"Never," said the innkeeper. "Perhaps she fears assassination."

"Perhaps," said the vizier.

Later, the small band of men gathered in the inn of Osiris.

"We must go into the pyramid and rescue Mira," Ariston said. When others protested, he added, "We will lure out the guards first. Then we will find the queen viper in her nest and cut off the head from the tail."

"You speak more truth than you know," said the vizier. "Here. Use this, when the time comes." And he passed a well-crafted silver mirror to the king. "You must set out just before dawn. If I am right, it may be the only way to defeat Jaramsheela."

The group set out for the pyramid as Obadiah instructed. According to Ariston's plans they laid their traps. Osiris lured a couple out from their guard posts with reports of having seen the fugitive. The guards came running, only to be ensnared by nets. The rebels slit the guards' throats, and they bled black upon the sand. Next, they hurried to the pyramid entrance. Ariston appeared weaponless, saying that he wanted to give himself up. As the guards surrounded him, hidden archers cut them down from the windows of the houses. They died without a sound.

The pyramid lay open before them.

The little force raced up the green jade passageways, hacking at all those who remained. Archers paved the way for Ariston. His sword sang once again in his strong stone fingers. They reached the inner chambers of the queen. With one stroke, Ariston cleaved the cedarwood door in twain,

Several guards rushed out to meet them. Ariston's sword drank greedily from their throats. It was only then that the true horror became known.

The queen lay on her throne, the body of Mira in her arms. The girl bled from the throat, her white skin and fluttering eyelids telling all too well that the story of her life was ended. The queen dropped the girl and wiped the blood from her lips.

Afrodicius came between them. Though not as powerfully built as Ariston, yet he twirled a fighting dagger and a shortsword with expert grace.

Wary, the pair circled. Afrodicius's short blade sword whipped through the air, as his other hand slashed out with his poniard, scoring a crimson line across Ariston's chest. The king flinched not. Then the pair of them closed. What the king lacked for in speed now thanks to his jewelled hand he made up for in its awesome strength. The short blade snapped ineffectually against the glittering stone fingers. Afrodicius backed away, and now it was Ariston's turn, whirling his weapon in his hand, slicing down. Afrodicius jumping clear just in time as Ariston's blade hacked a brazier in twain. Afrodicius began to sweat as they danced across the throne room

Meanwhile Shem and his outlaws approached the queen. She smiled like a hyena surrounded by lions. They loosed their arrows, but the Queen caught them with her hands. Astonished, two of the men fled. But Shem knew this was no spectre, but a creature of flesh and blood. He drew his sword, forged in his own smithy, crude but ready for battle. He prepared to strike down the witch. Yet the Queen was faster; she caught his arm and plunged her right hand into his chest up to the wrist. With a hungry laugh, she let his lifeless body slump to the ground.

Afrodicius retreated up against the stone wall. His dagger had tasted Ariston's flesh many times. Yet still his opponent fought, not weary but faster, as though the battle was giving him strength. The king's face contorted into a ferocious mask of molten rage that would have frightened a starving lion. Afrodicius bent on one knee as blow upon blow rained down upon his shortsword. At length, the blade snapped in two, splintering under Ariston's broadsword.

Afrodicius knelt there, panting, sweating.

"Mercy?" Ariston said at last.

Afrodicius spat blood at Ariston's feet. "What do you know of mercy, you who bring chaos to the city where we had peace?"

"You had peace," Ariston said. "But it was bought at too high a price."

Without a moment's hesitation, he severed Afrodicius's head from his shoulders. The body fell forward and hit the floor. The head rolled away, the lips still moving, but silent now, without a throat to give it voice.

"You have done well, my king," Queen Jaramsheela said, an apparition in her white gown stained crimson. Ariston saw for the first time the bodies scattered around and marvelled. "You will be a worthy replacement for Afrodicius."

"You do not know me," said the king.

"I know all men, and I know all warriors. What is it they crave more than anything? Battle-glory and gore. What is a warrior without war? Come, and we will rule not just this kingdom, but the next. You may fight for me in my name, and we will make an empire to make all of history tremble."

Ariston saw the body of the girl, Mira, her throat savaged by wicked teeth. And he remembered what Obadiah had said. He glanced about. Far above, the old sun had arisen. A single ventilation shaft poked a finger of light through the ceiling, reaching down until it was consumed in the gloom. He felt behind him in the belt of his tunic for the silver mirror.

"A king to rule by your side? What's in it for you?"

"Not quite by my side, but close enough," Jaramsheela said. She drew close and encircled her arms about Ariston's neck. "Close enough so that you could be the power behind my throne. All you have to do is swear your love for me. Renounce any gods and we can rule together for a thousand years. Nay, more."

"A thousand years of cutting people's tongues out?"

"Many must be subjugated so that they might know peace at last," she said. "There is no room for those who speak out. All must declare their subservience, and in return I give them what they want. Final… peace."

Saying this, she opened her lips wide. A cold shudder ran through Ariston's weary limbs as he saw fangs, long like a viper's, coming for his throat. The arms grew vice-like around him, an iron padlock no man could break. And he understood how it was that Queen Jaramsheela remained young while so many grew old.

He thrust the mirror in her face.

The angled glass reflected the sunlight's thin beam onto her alabaster skin, skin that turned black as soon as the light beams struck. The queen screamed and withdrew, collapsing into herself like a slug covered in quicklime.

Steam hissed from her pale limbs. Her flesh grew brittle and grey. King Ariston angled the mirror so that she could not escape its golden wrath. She fled about the room, this way and that, but the light burned and scorched where it touched her. Flames erupted across her body. She cast her face up to the heavens, emitted one final scream, then her blackened flesh exploded like a stamped-out timber on a blazing bonfire.

The chamber grew silent once more.

Two shapes appeared at the entrance. Obadiah and Osiris. The innkeeper yelled out on seeing his son and daughter both dead. He cradled the girl in his arms and wept. Obadiah inspected the ashen remains of Jaramsheela and crushed one remaining hand beneath his silken slippers.

"Once I relished the sound of weeping," said Ariston. They watched the innkeeper lamenting his lost brood. "Now I care for it not."

He placed his jewelled hand upon the innkeeper's shoulder, but Osiris heard him not, lost in his own grief.

"Will you rule in her place, my lord? This is a fine city. Its people are not so bad. Once they regain their courage they'll make a fine fighting force."

Ariston surveyed the grim remains. He flexed the fingers of his jade hand.

"Not under me. I find I have little taste for kingship these days."

"And battle?"

The king gave his vizier a worldly grin. "Battle is another matter. There are many injustices in this world, and I have much to make up for. But I could use a friend by my side."

Obadiah nodded. "My old wits are ever at your disposal, my lord."

"Then let us go," Ariston said, leading the old vizier out of the dead queen's chamber. "This place stinks of death worse than any tomb."

And so saying, King Ariston and Obadiah the Vizier left Jabur to its own laments and ruminations, and swept out onto the wide plain, disappearing into the western sun and into history, like two small motes in the molten eye of God.

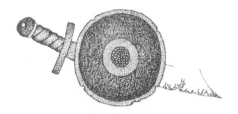

RED
Chadwick Ginther

Their home was in disarray. But then, it usually was. Red had never seen a more slovenly haberdasher than her brother, Needle.

Today was different. The building had been tossed. A queue of suspects paraded through her mind. Needle collected enemies and murder attempts the way most tailors did thread.

Dummies were strewn over the floor and bolts of cloth had been slashed and discarded. Red eased her sword from its scabbard. It had been the first real gift her brother had given her.

She kicked her sandals off and padded lightly through the room, checking corners, closets and piles of debris for any sign of who could have done this. Satisfied no one was waiting to follow her up the stairs, she crept to the second floor, avoiding the steps that creaked.

At the top of the landing, the door to their sleeping chamber was ajar. She waited, and listened. She held her breath; blood pulsed steadily in her ears. Red could hold her breath a long time. There were no tell-tale sounds of anyone within.

Red knelt with her sword to the bottom of the door. She moved it about, seeing nothing in the reflection.

Good enough.

She burst in and slid to the left as the door slammed against the wall. Her eyes flickered over the room. Their modest beds had been smashed, and the screen separating them was shattered.

There was a small pool of blood on the floor. Not enough to mean death, but not much to hang belief or hope upon. There was a pattern of score marks—like a spider's web—scratched into the floor. A cult symbol, maybe. But who carved it there? Needle, or his abductors? Needle may have been taken alive. Whether he stayed so would be up to her.

*

It was illegal to wear armour in Khyber, unless you were among the Watch. Armour had to have the appearance of being flimsy, mere ornamentation rather than protection. Caravan guards and cult bludgeons alike had learned little tricks to circumvent the restriction. So had Red.

She tightened the choker about her throat and threw a hood over her unruly short red curls. Her choker dangled thin, linked chains of copper—like fine chain mail. Not much protection, but it would stop a knife from drawing her a second smile. Red also had a thick leather shirt cinched up with laces. Again, not much. But hopefully enough to keep her in a fight.

The streets of the Goodson's Quarter were still and quiet. With Goodmass so close, the One God's faithful would be at the Wall at least until the sun had met its zenith. Red wound her way to the Diviners' Quarter, dropping bribes and tariffs to petty kings of petty kingdoms as she moved from quarter to quarter. She hoped she'd have enough coin left to pay a seer; Needle could be anywhere in the city and the sooner she was pointed towards him, the better Red would feel.

SWORDS & SORCERIES

*

Superstition held the only way to change one's pronounced future was to kill the seer whose lips had spoken it. As such, the seers were adamant that no weapons be allowed in their quarter, and so naturally, no one approached the Diviners unarmed.

Red was no different. She wore her sword in a baldric rather than at her waist, so it would be hidden by her cloak. She'd worn a dirk at her belt and slipped a throwing dagger into each tall boot. The knives had given her something for the guards to find, and something for her to hand over. It had taken more coin for the guards' search to stop there.

Khyber thieves were almost as adept at hiding weapons in plain sight as sellswords were at disguising their armour. Red had learned a few tricks from them, too. Needle had sewn lead shot into her gloves. A sling was wound into her belt, making a false drawstring at the front of her trousers. A bracelet of polished, globular stones gave her ammunition. Not good in an ambush, true, but it paid to have a backup weapon for when they started running. Red's silver pouch made a good blackjack in a pinch. Though the way she was dropping coin today, she may have to swing more than once.

Red's confidence was waning with every step she took into the Diviners' Quarter. As she walked down the Street of Dreams, seers, soothsayers, and prophets all hawked visions from tents and wooden antechambers built out into the streets from imposing stone buildings. She couldn't afford any future provided by the more prominent seers and with each cross street the prophets that followed seemed more disreputable than those before them.

"I see nothing," the first to take her coin said.

Another, "I see nothing."

Nothing, nothing, and more bloody nothing.

Wooden additions and pavilion tents gave way to rough awnings and shoddy lean-tos. She'd reached the wall marking the edge of the street, and the quarter. Now, madmen babbled at her with bald heads uncovered in the sun. Unwashed flesh wafted alongside forgotten fruit and rancid meat.

They paid no attention to her beyond their garbled words and animal howls. Perhaps she was merely part of another vision, to them. At the final stall Red stopped; the building had started to crumble. Fallen bricks had been stacked loosely around the entrance forming a short, curved wall.

"Divine Caro seeks those who are lost!" called a voice dripping with madness. "Divine Caro foresaw the rise of the Goodson and the sundering of Khyber."

Her first glimpse of the seer was a rooster comb of dark, unruly hair that rose behind the wall like the fin of a bloodfish.

"Divine" Caro was young, perhaps of an age with Red. *Saw the rise of the Goodson my freckled bottom.*

He regarded her through squinted eyes. "You, my dear, strike me as a woman not to be fucked with."

He saw well enough. And his apparent madness left quickly.

"You've hit the nail on the head with that strike, Divine One."

"As I have seen, so it shall be." Caro nodded vigorously. "Come, come."

The seer stood, a carpet of black hair swathing a skeleton body. He was naked and waved her to join him behind the wall.

Careful not to knock any of the unmortared bricks loose, Red sighed and stepped over the wall. She had no problem with putting a prick to its proper use, but why did every man seem to think she wanted to look at the silly thing?

"Sit, sit," Caro said, gesturing at a rounded rock as he sat upon another. "You are seeking someone?"

"I am," Red said slowly.

Caro smiled. "You must be truly desperate to have walked so far into the dream."

"Your... colleagues saw nothing."

Caro brushed a hand over Red's gloves. "Perhaps because you are armed, against all custom."

Catching the seer's hand and crushing it in a tight grip, Red pulled him close and whispered, "Is it not also customary to kill the speaker of a grim prophecy, so it may not find you?"

Caro loosed a throaty chuckle. "That it is, that it is. Now that we understand one another, whom do you seek? Brother? Husband? Father? *Lover?*"

"Brother."

"Pity," he said with a pout. "He has a name? This brother of yours?"

"Needle."

"Then I cannot help you."

"Why not?"

Caro sighed. He looked sad. "Telling you will do you little good, my lovely. There is no road to reach him. He is buried so deeply, not even the Ferryman could take you to him in time."

*

Red didn't know the Ferryman, Khyber's god of the underworld, but she did know *a* ferryman. Maybe the Keeper of the Floating Dock could get her there.

The Dock of Floating Doors was a gateway to anywhere in Khyber—if you had the coin. And the stones. Needle knew the Keeper of the Floating Dock better than Red. So she had to hope the little bugger didn't owe the Keeper any coin. Otherwise she'd need her blade for a key.

Red ducked into an alley. Xenia's shop wasn't the nearest entrance to the Floating Dock, but she was the only Keeper's Steward Red knew who *might* also talk about who had taken Needle. All kinds passed through her shop and she heard a great many things she might share for the proper silver. If Xenia could help her, Red mightn't need to deal with the Keeper at all. And if X couldn't help, at least she'd be right where she needed to be.

There was no shingle to announce the shop. If Xenia didn't already know you, she didn't want to know you. Red pushed the door open; the merry chime of a bell didn't quite hide the click of a crossbow bolt being locked in place.

"X, it's me," Red said, holding her hands away from her sword.

"I have eyes," the Xiou woman said. "And they still see."

Red stepped into the shop and nudged the door shut with her foot. Xenia may have taken an Andaran name, but the woman dressed in the fine silks of her folk far to the east.

"Do they see well enough for you to put your shanker down?"

"Depends," Xenia said, "on why you're here."

"Needle. He's missing."

"Why are you even looking?" Xenia asked. "He cheats at cards. Cheats at dice. Cheats on women."

Xenia *was* right, Needle was a cheat. But that wasn't the whole of what he was, either. He was kind to Red. And charming. His charm could be painful in its own way, his quick hands twirling a stiletto, his quicker mouth saying,

"They don't call me Needle for the blade in my pants, luv."

"He's the only family I've got. And I mean to keep him." Red had a reputation as the best woman with a blade in Khyber. And Xenia knew better than to push her. "Found a symbol like a spider's web, carved on the floor. Mean anything to you?"

"Tala's Web," Xenia said, turning.

So it *was* one of the cults. Since the Potent had moved his court—taking much of the Goodson's faithful with him—the various cults dwelling in Khyber's shadows came out of hiding, blinked at the daylight, and carved out their own little territories. Needle had once tried to catalogue them all. "The better to shirk their tariffs," he'd told her.

Tala's Web. Red knew the name but not much else.

"Tell me of them."

"They're old. Very old," Xenia said. "Tala was spinning her silken web in Xiou long before your Goodson was hung from the Wall; before Andar or his empire were birthed. Her brood has been growing since the Potent abandoned Khyber."

"Let me guess: they want the entire city for themselves?" Xenia nodded.

"So why Needle?"

"He knows too much. Knowledge worth more than his dirk—or his stitches."

Red sighed and turned her back to Xenia, feigning interest in the narcotics and potions neatly lined on rough shelves.

Khyber's cults got along well enough, provided they stayed within their own territories. There were skirmishes now and again, but nothing larger than that in decades. Tala's Web would have open warfare on every street in Khyber.

Red heard the whistle of a club just in time to duck her head. It rang off her crown and she groaned, faking a slump towards the floor. Her hood had a padded cap sewn within—another rogue's trick. She'd see stars for a moment, but without it, Xenia would have staved in her skull.

As Red dropped, she rolled to the side. Xenia's second strike was overbalanced. Red shot to her feet, grabbed the Xiou woman by the hair and slammed her face into the counter. She pulled a blade from Xenia's belt and put it to the woman's throat.

"Now," Red growled. "Talk."

*

Red had been lucky. Tala's Web wanted Needle alive. Xenia hadn't known why, or where they squatted. That meant Red would have to barter with the Keeper directly. An unpleasant task at the best of times. But those who chose to move about the Undercity couldn't exactly complain to the Watch or Lord General about his prices.

Behind Xenia's counter was a trap door that led into the Undercity of Khyber. The bones of the Andaran Empire had shouldered modern Khyber for centuries. Many of those ruins had flooded. Honest folk these days used them for either cistern or sewer. To less honest folk, the Keeper and his ferrymen provided an equally necessary service— transportation across caste and cult boundaries. At the base of the steps were a smouldering brazier and the chimes and dried lilies with which to summon him.

To Red's surprise, he was waiting for her atop his skiff. Nothing of his face was visible in the lantern light, save his white smile. He watched impassively as Red dumped Xenia's corpse into the water.

"I've been expecting you," he said, finally. He beckoned her to join him. Red stood her ground. The Keeper let out a long, hissing breath. "You should have come to me first. Your brother would weep at your hesitation."

Red snorted. "He'd weep at the thought I was stupid enough to join you without discussing payment." *Or safe return.*

"What is there to discuss?" he asked. "You spent your coin on foolish seers. You cannot afford to be taken where you want to go."

The seers had shaved her for near every silver she'd had and given nothing in return. Red cursed inwardly. If he knew about that, he probably knew where her offering had come from, but she hoped X's silver would tip the Keeper's scales.

"So take me where I *need* to go," she said, holding up the coin.

"Bargaining with coin that belongs to me?" the Keeper chided. "And if your needs take you away from your brother?"

"They won't."

The Keeper's smile glowed, matching the corpsecandle light of his skiff's lantern. "So certain."

"So doubtful."

The Keeper of the Dock laughed. The sound was arid and breathy, possessing as much mirth and goodwill as the Garan desert.

"You have *sand*, Redala," he said, nodding. "I will take you where you need to go."

The Keeper took Red's hand in his; it was rough and dry, and had the sensation of a manacle snapping shut. He guided her onto his skiff and pushed away from the dock. Grim shadows devoured the weak light from his lantern. He whispered a tuneless song as he poled towards an older tunnel. It took Red a moment to recognize the song, and when she did, she shivered. It had been the dirge from her parents' funeral.

At first, Red had tried to keep track of their passage. But on occasion, the Keeper would shutter his lantern, making the task impossible. In those moments, she felt a twinge in her belly, like she was folding in on herself.

"There are things in the dark, Redala," he whispered. "That would risk the light for even such old and spoiled meat as I. For you, they would risk much, much more."

Red bit her tongue; she didn't trust herself to speak. The skiff creaked and rocked. He poled further into the dark and Red grew anxious. It was an interminable wait. Finally, he unshuttered the lantern and gave her a curt nod.

"We are here," he said, holding them steady by jamming his pole into what had once been a doorframe. "Where you *need* to be."

There were two steps leading up to the doorway. Red hopped from the skiff to the landing, not waiting for the Keeper's offer of assistance.

She steadied herself and waited for her pounding heart to slow to a quiet pulse. A sound, distant and familiar, dredged up from memory greeted her in the silence. Soft, echoing drops, water falling from a great height into a vast pool. She had been here before.

The Keeper slid his lantern down the length of his skiff pole, letting it drop to the stone floor with a quiet thud.

"Because we are so friendly," he said. "You may consider that assistance free."

Yeah, right.

Red snatched the lantern and held it aloft. The room's ceiling vaulted well above its meagre light. She could see

181

neither the end of the chamber nor the walls to either side of her. Innumerable pillars stretched into the yawning darkness.

It was the Potent's Cistern. Before he'd fled Khyber, this had been the personal water supply of the Speaker for the Word of God.

"Now," the Keeper said slowly. "You know where you are. You know where you need to go."

If the Keeper had brought her here, there was only one place that Needle—and Tala's Web—could be.

The eager darkness swallowed her up as the Keeper poled his skiff away. Something splashed far in the distance. There were fish that lived in these cisterns. Fish and . . . worse.

Red and Needle used to swim in these pools when they were children. They'd mapped out entire series of linked vaults, some of which could only be accessed after a long and harrowing swim through sunken, water-filled tunnels.

She was less concerned about holding her breath than she was with getting stuck. The skinny wriggler who'd swam these passages with her brother was long gone. Now Red swam the ocean span of the Khyber isthmus for strength and endurance. She was a strong swimmer, a skill that had been forced upon her. Her swordmaster had pushed her into the filthy harbour and swore she'd never touch a blade until she could swim the span between the two Pillars. "Your arms are weak," he'd said. "And you suck air like a bellows."

No longer.

Red was near the height of a Valkuran male, a good head taller than most men in Khyber. A child's body had been replaced with lean, corded muscle.

She sighed as she stripped out of shirt and pants. She left on her smallclothes and a light band of fabric over her breasts. She wasn't modest, but Needle wouldn't be seeing her naked body, the dirty whoreson.

Red took X's knife from her boot and tied it round one ankle. She also kept her choker on. While she dearly wanted to bring her sword, there was no way she could carry it and still swim the connecting tunnels. Still, she hated the idea of leaving it behind.

Dragging it behind her wouldn't work. She had neither rope nor cord but she wouldn't be returning for her clothes. She shredded her pants and knotted a line together.

Red tried to remember how many breaths it was to cross the longest submerged section of tunnels. It might be possible. She might drown for its weight, but she also didn't want to die for lack of a real blade. Knives were rarely enough for the kind of trouble Needle dragged her into.

She knew nothing of Tala's Web's numbers, nor how they'd be armed.

This wouldn't be the first time she'd been a fool over Needle.

Red tied her makeshift line around the quillons of her sword and knotted it tightly. She swaddled the length of the blade; she would need to cradle the sword to her body until she'd swam the length of the cistern. It wouldn't do to cut herself before she'd had a chance to start fighting.

She eased herself into the tepid water slowly, and pushed off from the stone landing. Swimming backstroke she could watch the lantern to mark her position.

Her sword was a strangely comforting weight on her breast. It filled the hollow in her gut that told her Needle was already dead.

It would be hard to silence such thoughts at the best of times. Now, alone in the darkness, with only a shrinking light to guide her, grim feelings were not easily banished.

She swam carefully, slowly, so as not to make much noise. Far off in the darkness there was a loud splash. Her every breath felt like a thunderclap as she kept her eyes locked on the lantern.

Another splash.

Closer.

How lucky Red and Needle had been to survive their exploring hadn't been impressed upon them until long after they'd left childish games behind — to take up the more dangerous games of adults. But Red remembered those days fondly still.

After their parents had died, Needle had urged her to keep her memory of the Undercity fresh. That someday their knowledge of the cisterns below Khyber might mean the difference between life and death.

She'd walked and swam this path in her mind many times. Red reached the far wall as the lantern burned itself out. She was alone in the black again. The waters of the cistern were far too deep for her to touch bottom and rest.

Something firm and sucking licked over her calf. Red eased her knife from its sheath and jabbed into the unseen thing. What had gripped her retreated and the water exploded into a flurry of splashes.

Red pawed in the dark; the stairs were still there and so was the hole to the next chamber. She crawled through, hissing softly as she scraped a knee over the broken brick. It was much tighter than she'd remembered. Red dropped into the next flooded chamber, sloshing a small spurt of water through the hole to run down the stairs and into the cistern below.

Here she could walk; the water was only to her waist. She paced through the steps in her memory. If this was the right passage, there should be a statue nearby. Red reached out blindly, waiting for her fingers to touch stone. She found it.

It had been a statue of Andar, founder of the city that came to be known as Khyber. Over the years, the image's erect phallus had been broken off. *So much for sowing the seeds of empire.*

Andar cradled her sword while she probed the next passage. In case the way was blocked, she didn't want to be fighting her blade as well.

There was a splash behind her. Bricks broke and tumbled into the chamber. The thing was still coming for her.

Now or never.

Red unwrapped her sword and tied the free end of the line to her ankle. She dropped her sword at the base of the tunnel. She gathered her breath in short, shallow bursts before filling her lungs to capacity, and dove down the hole in the floor. Bubbles of air tickled at her cheeks as Red slowly exhaled and felt ahead with her fingers.

Every time her toes brushed the line Red felt a surge of panic that it would tangle her feet. Every second, every kick, every breath was precious. It meant not just her life, but Needle's.

The tunnel narrowed further. She would not be able to turn now if the way were shut. Had she really grown so much since she'd first explored the Undercity?

Brick scratched Red's shoulders as she wormed her way through a pinch in the shaft, dragging herself forward as she kicked her feet. She almost screamed. Thrashing, she earned more scrapes on tender skin. This was the first time she'd ever regretted her sword training.

The darkness of the shaft pressed in on her. Pressure built in her ears. Behind her eyes. More bubbles rushed past her face. Something sharp bit into her shoulder and her kicking foot caught the line tethering her sword. There in the dark, her air dwindling, the tether and the drag of the sword, felt like the touch of the thing in the cistern.

Red pushed ahead, fighting an urge to exhale. Had the pinch and the moment of panic cost her too much air? She couldn't know. Not until it was too late

There was light above. There shouldn't be light above. A trick of eyes or mind? The tunnel melted away as she pulled herself to the surface. Her chest ached. If she didn't breach the water soon, she'd be fish food.

She kicked and felt a wrench in her hip and ankle. Her sword was caught. Red strained for the surface. The light grew no closer. The last of her air bubbled past her face. Light. Air. Her heart thudded in her breast. Blood pounded in her ears.

Panic.

Fight.

Submission.

Red slipped back down to the tunnel. Trying to move her legs and arms was like swinging lead. Black edged her vision, and Red saw Needle's grinning face. "Come on, luv," he seemed to say. "Don't keep me waiting."

He was dead already. She'd been fooling herself. If they saw one another again, it would be in the lichhouse.

Something sharp bit into her hand. Crushing it closed against the pain, Red hoped this would fuel her enough to reach air.

But the waiting dark claimed her.

*

Red spat up water and gulped a deep, racking breath. Surprised to have breath at all, she didn't care that there was light where there should be none. Didn't care who might see or hear her. A hand rested upon her aching chest, holding her to cold stone.

Feeling a stranger's breath pass her lips, Red balled her fist and swung. There was a deep, surprised grunt as she connected. Using the force of her strike, she rolled atop the man, cracking his head against the stone. With a moan, he went still.

When she'd filled her lungs and steadied her heart, Red noticed she was in a much smaller cistern. Two torches in sconces on the far wall illuminated the entire chamber. Steps led up and out. At the base of the steps was a rough wooden stool with a fisher's pole at its feet. A line of braided gut ran from the pole to a barbed hook in Red's palm.

At least one of Khyber's gods had been smiling on her. The fisher had brought up her blade with her.

Red had her life. She had her sword. Now she just needed Needle. She wondered if the nameless man knew of the sliding door at the far end of the cistern. It was invisible from this side, unless one knew what to look for. Red slid a torch from the wall, and whispered thanks to the fisher god, wishing she could give his servant more than an aching skull for his efforts, and eased the door closed behind her.

*

Beyond the cistern, sounds trilled in the darkness; echoing, groaning, shuddering the black. The water had been diverted somewhere else, and Red walked through dry—if refuse-filled—tunnels.

A sick, green light crept towards her from the far end of the passage. It would swallow the light from her torch; she may yet surprise them. She burned the sticky strands of spider's webbing with her torch sending the vermin to scurry into dark holes and recesses in the walls.

The tunnel opened up into a large chamber. Red had expected this chamber, like so much else in the Undercity, to have felt smaller, now that she was grown and walking the steps of memory in the flesh. And it did, but for different reasons.

Thick strands of fibrous webbing covered every surface but the floor. Desiccated bodies—animal and human—dotted the web like jewels on a feast day gown and the smell wafting from them would choke an undertaker. Shadowed tunnels honeycombed the great chamber. Hanging from the ceiling were many glowing, softly pulsating sacks. And Needle.

He was naked, strung up over an altar by his wrists and ankles. His chest rose and fell. Slowly, and shallowly. But he lived. She wasn't too late.

The light cast by the sacks lit the chamber completely. Shadows moved within. She shuddered. Eggs.

Tala didn't mean to *rule* Khyber. She meant to *eat* Khyber.

The cultists, dressed in filmy robes made from the same webs draping the chamber, had their backs to her. They busied themselves with some arcane preparations. Their chants grew louder, and from deep in one of the webbed-off tunnels echoed someone's death cry.

A knife in the back was more her brother's style than Red's. But she let her dagger fly anyway since he was too trussed up to do the deed.

She followed the dagger's wake. It thudded into a cultist's back and she sheared his head free before he could draw steel. His fellows turned to face her. Two women and one man.

The man yelled out; Red recognized the tone if not the words.

While the women moved to Red's flanks, the man advanced, a metal cudgel in his hand. Red jabbed her torch at the woman on her left. The cultist didn't even try to dodge. Her filmy garment caught fire immediately. She shrieked, but her frantic efforts only fuelled the flames. Sizzling meat and the stink of burning hair filled Red's nostrils.

Red turned from the stink and cries. Another cultist, his cloak making him invisible against the webbed walls of Tala's lair, thudded into Red. The impact staggered her. Only for a moment, but a moment was eternity in a fight.

A cord slipped over Red's head and tightened against her throat. The second woman was trying to garrotte her. Her choker kept it from digging into her flesh, but she knew her windpipe would be crushed eventually. If the man didn't brain Red first.

She couldn't risk using the torch—this close she'd only burn herself and her sword was no good for this engagement. The man's cudgel rose. Red waited. She was bigger than the woman strangling her. Stronger. The cudgel fell and Red dove forward bringing the woman riding up on her back. She felt the thud as the cudgel hit. The garrotte loosened and the woman tumbled to the floor.

Red gasped a quick breath and slid to the side. Her sword bit into a cultist's flank. She reversed the blade in time to parry the second man's next strike. From behind him there came another scream.

Skittering steps grew closer, and what emerged from the tunnel was not human, though it had made some attempts to paint such a shape. What crawled atop the webbing could have been a woman—were it not for the four chitinous limbs sprouting from her ribs and hips.

Tala.

In awe, the cultists dropped to their knees. They made no move to even block Red's killing stroke.

The goddess skittered closer to Needle. Mandibles pushed out from her mouth, splitting the skin of her human cheeks. Other prongs of sharp chitin pushed free from more unexpected, softer places. Red shuddered. She'd had no fear of spiders before this. She doubted she'd be able to say the same tomorrow. This scene would stalk her dreams for many a moon. Even Needle would balk at docking in *that* port.

Tala drooled something foul over Needle. He shuddered and convulsed, which, given his nakedness, was another sight that would stay with Red for too long.

She hurled the torch into the webs as she rushed forward. Tala's nest caught like flash powder and flames rushed into the chamber. There wouldn't be long for her to rescue Needle before the fire suffocated them.

The goddess squealed and dropped from her web, vaulting awkwardly on her spider's legs, trying desperately to save the glowing egg sacks.

Red reached Needle as Tala's squeals died amongst the hissing and popping of her burning children. Her brother was still completely senseless—admittedly no new state for him. Red hacked at the thick webs binding him and dragged him from the room as greasy, black smoke started to choke her.

Whatever Tala had spat up on him, Red wanted it off. Needle sputtered and swore when she made it back to the nearest cistern and hurled him into the water. Until he'd noticed his state of undress—and Red's.

"Lot of bother to get my clothes off, Red," Needle said.

She smiled. "If I'd known you were going to be naked, I would've stayed home."

Red splashed in after him, rinsing blood and strands of web off her body.

"I was to be wed to the spider goddess, luv," Needle said, beaming a drunken smile.

"She devours her mates, you blockhead."

Needle's eyes widened. "Before or after?"

"During," Red said.

The little thief considered her words. He shrugged. "Could be worse, yeah?"

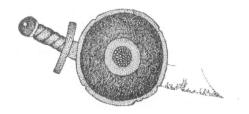

THE RECONSTRUCTED GOD
Adrian Cole

A familiar is granted a significant amount of freedom by its master in order to discharge the duties set for it by that master, and can, for example, trawl the depths of the astral realms that link the many dimensions of the omniverse. Single-minded creatures, familiars enjoy the protection, physical and supernatural, of their controlling superiors, and it would be a rare thing for a familiar to follow its own course, outside the constraints of a guiding hand. Indeed, without a master, a familiar is a doomed thing, destined to wink out of existence should it persist in rejecting the advances of sorcerers, mages and wizards who would anchor it to their cause.

Elfloq knew all this, of course. Yet, obtusely, he had selected for himself a master, in direct contrast to the accepted procedures in these matters. Not only that, but he had decided upon a particularly dark and devious being, one who had been banished by god and man alike, a being with whom any association invariably resulted in consequences only a fool would tempt.

Elfloq, was no fool, but his desire to serve the Voidal, for such was that being of eternal night, overrode all other emotions within his tiny breast. Elfloq had tasted his powers, and, like one snared by the most puissant of drugs, was committed to finding and serving only him. Inevitably it led him to strange and dangerous realms.

*

"There are keys and there are keys," said the traveller. He was a man of indistinct bulk, given that he had wrapped himself in so many robes that his physical outline was smothered. This habiliment was many-coloured, resplendent in fact, and served well its purpose in attracting companions to him in the Inn of Bright Beginnings. Indeed, the traveller was such a brilliant advertisement for the place that its hosts, the sparkling Grinningwit Brothers, encouraged his visits by supplementing his food and drink with frequent offerings on the house. Aggrabal the Aesthete, for so the traveller named himself, was always to be found at the centre of things in the inn, surrounded by admirers of one persuasion or another. He was a great one for barter, often exchanging something, be it a solid trinket or a stirring tale, an invaluable tome or a slip of information vital to someone's cause. And there was always much singing, shouting and carousing around him.

Elfloq had come to the sprawling city of Melliflusia-in-the-Mist at the suggestion of an old colleague, another familiar he had met by pure chance out in the astral realms. "Wonderful place," he had been told. "Never a dull moment. Always a nugget or two to be found there. I'd start with the aptly named Inn of Bright Beginnings. A positive trove of knowledge."

Squatting high up on a beam as he now did, Elfloq observed the delighted mayhem below him in the inn's great hall. Bodies heaved, voices roared, faces smiled, and the world spun happily on its axis. Aggrabal was directly below, looking exactly as he had been described to Elfloq. His voice, sharp and commanding, cut through the noise and the people crammed together around him listened attentively, like children hearing the most exciting of tales.

"There are keys and there are keys," Aggrabal repeated.

"I have a sackful tethered to my steed, back at the stable. What places they open! Beware, though, should you think to slip out and attempt to pilfer my treasures. Some of those keys will open doorways to doom and disaster, and who can tell which is which? Would you risk your eternal soul, for that is the cost of error. The Key of Keys itself might be among them, but even should you find it, can you control its stunning powers?"

Elfloq's ears picked up. Key of Keys? What was this? He had heard not a whisper, not a hint of this thing. An item of great power, by the sound of it. That, or a trick of the traveller, a means of protecting his hoard. He listened attentively, but for now the traveller busied himself telling other tales, conducting his standard business, and although much of what he said, and at times sang, was fascinating and clearly of profound interest to the crowd, Elfloq heard nothing more to inspire him, and no further reference to the Key of Keys.

In his wanderings, Elfloq had honed the art of being patient to a master craft, even when ennui threatened to engulf him. It was a long time before Aggrabal concluded his business for the day and was allowed by his reluctant admirers to quit the hall. There were a few stragglers, intent on gleaning a last morsel from the traveller, but at last he was able to head for his lodgings. These were discreet and quiet, as the Inn of New Beginnings would have been no place to attempt to rest for a man in such demand.

Elfloq slipped across rooftops and between chimneys, shadowing the man, invisible and silent as a spectre. Satisfied that Aggrabal had retired for the night, Elfloq made a cursory inspection of the outer walls and windows of the inconspicuous inn where Aggrabal had bedded down. It was a simple matter for the familiar to fly up to an open window and slip on to its ledge, merging with the stonework. Peering inside the darkened room, Elfloq saw that the traveller was already fast asleep, having exhausted himself.

Elfloq dropped down on to the floor and sat himself at the end of the bed, light as a fly. Aggrabal opened one eye, which gleamed with reflected light from the single candle that guttered in its stand beside the bed. The eye fixed on the odd shape before it. It saw a being less than half the size of a man, a squamous, squat creature, with a batrachian head and features, thin, membranous wings folded behind it.

"A familiar!" he said, sitting up with a smile that suggested he was not afraid of such beings. "Has someone sent you to propose a contract with me? Splendid. Never mind the hour, nor that I am weary."

Elfloq smiled. That is to say, his face shaped an expression that was designed to be a smile, but not being human, it resembled a grimace. "Exalted one, most highly esteemed among traders -"

"Spare me the flattery, little familiar! I know how this goes." Aggrabal chuckled, and it was a genuinely warm sound. "Who sent you?"

"I was merely passing through the city and by pure chance I -"

Aggrabal's chuckle became an outright laugh. "Nonsense! You're a familiar. You're not blown about by the winds of chance. Who are you?"

"I am Elfloq."

"And your master is?"

Elfloq squirmed, "I find myself temporarily on the cusp-"

"Oh dear. Last one passed on? Left you out on a limb?"

"In a manner of speaking -"

"Never mind. Discretion is my watchword. So what do you want with me?"

"To help me reunite with my master. He is no ordinary sorcerer. Indeed, not a sorcerer at all. Not a wizard, or mage, or spellmaster."

"Does he have a name?"

"Yes, but it's not a name I care to speak casually. There are consequences to such actions." Elfloq mentally cursed himself for making the confession. It may yet serve to undermine his plans.

"You want me to help you find him, this nameless being? He has powers, I take it? Would they, by any chance, be dark and questionable? Has your master been banned, excommunicated, thrust out into the darker regions or otherwise banished?"

Elfloq fidgeted as he attempted to find the appropriate words to wriggle out of this verbal predicament. This trader was quick witted and shrewd.

"I see by your agitation that he has," said Aggrabal. "Well, I'm not sure that I would want to dare any reprisals attached to the assistance of such a dark being. There would obviously be significant risks involved. What's in it for me?"

"If you should summon my master, your rewards would be immense. He would make you an emperor among traders. In all the dimensions, no one would match you. You could trade entire worlds -"

Once again Aggrabal cut the little figure off in mid-sentence. "That's preposterous! Only the gods bestow such powers, and on very rare occasions do they favour a mortal, such as I am, with those kind of extravagant gifts. Wait – I begin to see. You serve such a god. A banished god, is it? The picture defines itself more clearly. Such a god would have enemies, rivals, would he not?"

"As do we all -"

"Yes, but I would rather avoid stirring up a pack of angry deities. I say again, who is your master?"

"He has many names."

"Give me one!"

"Some call him Fatecaster. Others, he who walks in the void, while others -"

Aggrabal's look of absolute horror was fearful enough to silence Elfloq. The trader gaped. "The *void*? You're telling me your master is – no, I'll not speak his name. Or summon him! Fires of the Burning Hells of Mundathusiar! You almost tricked me there, monster! Don't waste any more of my time. Begone!"

"Wait, wait," said Elfloq. "You are far too hasty, master."

"Really? I know enough forbidden knowledge to understand that anyone insane enough to summon the – your master – would indeed be well rewarded, but the price to be paid would ultimately be horrible beyond contemplation. Death itself would be a relief. No, no, you'll not hook me into your nefarious plans."

For a while the two of them were motionless, lost in thought. Elfloq realized he had little hope of striking any kind of bargain with this clever trader. The man was obviously every bit as devious, slippery and oblique as he was.

"Perhaps there is a compromise to be reached here."

Elfloq's bulbous eyes narrowed, his suspicions immediately aroused. "Oh?"

"I have no intention of summoning your master. If that is your unshakable goal, then you must find some other deluded being to sacrifice. However, there are other things I can provide you with that might aid you in your quest. You wish to be reunited with your master."

"That is my only desire."

"There may be other ways to reach him besides the ritual of summoning him. Had you thought of that? No, probably not. The omniverse is full of hidden paths, many of them lost or hidden, forbidden to the uninitiated. What you need, my friend, is a key."

Elfloq's ears pricked up. It was mention of the Key of Keys that had attracted him to the trader in the first place. "You possess such a thing?"

"As it happens, I do. You may have heard me speak in the Inn of Bright Beginnings of the Key of Keys. Its appearance is deceptive, for it looks singularly ordinary, with nothing to distinguish it as remarkable. I have it tucked away inside a sack that is filled with similarly bland-looking keys. A precaution against thieves."

"This key could unlock the door to the path to my master?"

"Undoubtedly. With it you could find your way to the feet of the Dark Gods themselves."

"That would not be my intention."

"A wise consideration. So – you want the key?"

Elfloq attempted to look nonchalant, but his efforts were doomed to failure. "You have a price in mind, of course?"

Aggrabal smiled, his brilliant white teeth like the jaws of a trap. "Naturally. Would you expect less of me? But it would not be beyond your means."

"Name it. You understand, I retain the right of refusal. This is not a verbal contract we are entering into. Nothing binding until I have considered the price."

"My, you are a cautious one! But that's fine. I will *loan* you the key for a specified period of time. During that time, you may do with it as you please. Also, you will serve me. I will be your temporary master in all things, saving your primary cause. You will remain free to pursue that cause, provided I am not compromised in any way."

"How long is this pact to be binding?"

"Shall we say, three days? With an option to extend."

Usually Elfloq would have haggled for as long as it took to gain a better advantage, but he had the distinct feeling that if he did so, he'd lose out, so after a short mental deliberation, he acceded. Three days it was.

*

The candle burned low as night passed, silent as thought, and Elfloq listened to Aggrabal as he quietly but animatedly expounded his expectations and the part he desired the familiar to play in them.

"So you see, Elfloq, I have but one fragment of this reconstruction to obtain. One simple piece and the picture is complete."

"So, in summary?"

"For some time now, I have been engaged in a quest. It relates to a god, a minor deity that few would be aware of outside the remote realm in which he once exercised his divine will. For convenience I have named him Uzbandazra, a suitable alias, designed to confuse anyone who might try to poke an unwanted nose into my affairs. Like many of his kind, his aspirations outgrew his abilities and he infuriated a pantheon of far more powerful gods. Never mind the details."

Elfloq knew this was a common failing among gods, regardless of their importance.

"Uzbandazra, for his sins, was stripped of his powers and dispersed. Physically. The angry gods literally dismantled him as though he were no more than a statue, as a mark of their contempt. No one thought any more of the matter and Uzbandazra was forgotten, ceasing to exist, and with him his powers. The sorrowful story would have ended there, but for a chance discovery. I happened to be involved in a particularly lively auction in Zeem, the Shifting City, a place which has often rewarded me in the past with priceless books, artifacts and wonders. Here I made a very reasonable bid for one such item, namely a part of an unusual statue. Probably no one else understood its true value, or nature, but something about it touched a nerve in me."

"A foot," said Elfloq. "You won a statue's foot."

"That is so. And as I have said, I went on to find more individual segments of the statue, scattered near and far throughout the numerous dimensions of the omniverse. It has taken me an age, but my quest for completion is almost over. One fragment remains, and then I shall own the reconstructed god!"

"You neglected to say what you intend to do with it."

"Revive the god, of course! Can you imagine how grateful such a being would be! I would attain powers second only to the god, for certain. Immortality, perhaps. There's no limit to the possibilities."

"Quite," said Elfloq. "And you want me to find the missing fragment, the final piece."

"That would be your task."

"In three days?"

"That's all it will take."

"So you know what it is, and where it is?"

"Yes, on both accounts. It is a jewel, a ruby of sorts. Larger than usual, but certainly not so large that a small familiar like yourself could not carry it in a suitable sack. It is the very heart of Uzbandazra. Once set in place, it will beat again."

"If it is in Zeem, why do you not go there yourself and-"

"Oh, no. It is not there. Each piece of the god was placed in a unique spot. The ruby is elsewhere. Unfortunately, it is in a realm that I am not able to visit. Previously I was involved in a – ah, dispute, with the Oligarchs of Perpetual Command, the rulers of the realm. They accused me – falsely, you understand, of thieving. Thieving! I simply outwitted them in a small matter of barter. I escaped intact from their churlish vengeance, but not before they had triple-cursed me and warned me my return would not end well for me. In short, a fate awaits me there not unlike that meted out to Uzbandazra. And unlike him, once I am dispersed, I could not be reassembled and reanimated."

"I see my part in this. I am to go there and purloin the ruby. I have three days to do this, after which you will loan me the Key of Keys."

"Not quite. You'll have the key at the outset, and for the three-day duration. After that, it will return to me. It's part of its power. So don't think you can run off with it. Make good use of it while you can. Those who went before you, sadly, did not."

Elfloq scowled deeply. "Those who went before?"

"It's only fair to warn you, you are the nineteenth assistant I've sent on this quest. The Oligarchs of Perpetual Command have disposed of all the others. All that came back to me was the Key of Keys. I'd have gladly exchanged it for the ruby, but apparently the rulers will not consider parting with it. They claim it is the organ of all their powers. So you'll need to be circumspect."

Elfloq's frightful scowl deepened. He tried to recall if the number twenty had any specific magical properties. He was still reflecting on that as the sun's first rays appeared over the city skyline.

*

Elfloq's eager mind and quick wits had him dreaming up and discarding a number of very devious plans before he eventually quit the city of Melliflusia-in-the-Mist. By then he had settled on his cunning plot, and felt rather pleased with himself at its ingenuity. His first port of call would be the private haggling house of the renowned jeweller, Thorgobrund. There were deals to make with him, and desires to be fuelled.

And so it was. Having made his representations, set out his stall and concluded his agreements with Thorgobrund, Elfloq set out once more, prepared now to tackle the more dangerous part of his quest. Arriving in the grim, compact realm of Dizzirambis, home of the Oligarchs of Perpetual Command, he dropped furtively from the air and alighted on a rough tower of stone, a deserted spot, some distance from what appeared to be a sprawling metropolis. It was twilight and the road beneath him was empty, the plain before the city silent and motionless, dusty and rutted. Now and then a cart rumbled out of the surrounding hills and headed toward the huge city gates. Elfloq decided that although to fly over the great walls would have been a simple matter, there could well be guards, mortal or supernatural, watching over the parapets. Easier to slip aboard one of the larger carts and secrete himself within its crates and boxes, with which most seemed to be laden.

Night was about to wrap the city in its clammy folds by the time Elfloq had ensconced himself up in the roofs of the city, where smoke boiled among sooty stacks in a cramped, tiled landscape where few, if any, of the inhabitants resided. Elfloq considered what he'd been told by Aggrabal. The Palace of Perpetuity was where the trader knew the object of his desire was to be found. *Don't be confused*, he had said. *It is not a salubrious building. Quite the reverse. It's hidden among numerous garish and bungled architectural disasters, disguising it from prying eyes. The Oligarchs are famously secretive and have a ludicrously inflated sense of their own importance.*

Elfloq assumed, however, that the Oligarchs were not without power, hence the trader's dilemma. The familiar flitted to and fro, disturbing a number of shadowy, irritated creatures from their night perches, but for now his progress was unimpeded. The Palace of Perpetuity, he had been told, was to be found in the north of the city, on higher ground, so that its own towers and minarets could look out over Dizzirambis on those occasions when the fog and billowing smoke did not smother it. Elfloq would have cursed the filthy air, but consoled himself with the fact that his intrusion was well cloaked.

Before long he espied his goal. It had the appearance of a huge ziggurat that had once reached up to the heavens, but which had succumbed to the pressures of its own weight and partially collapsed, with the result that half of its upper walls and towers leaned like the masts of ships in a churning sea swell, bound to topple at any moment. Such a dangerous structure would have deterred most of the populace, high born or otherwise from a desire to be anywhere remotely near it, but from Aggrabal's words, the Oligarchs were more than content to obscure themselves in its state of imminent collapse. No doubt, Elfloq told himself, though not convincingly, the Oligarchs' powers were sufficient to shore the place up.

The familiar made the final swoop across a curdling sky and alighted on a parapet that had the consistency of lightly baked cake. Elfloq had to flit upwards quickly as part of the parapet instantly dissolved under even his slight weight. It took him a number of attempts to find somewhere here where he could set down without causing a minor disaster. Once he had done so, he found himself face to face with a creature of about the same height as he was, though it was considerably bulkier. It peered at him from pinpoint eyes and sniffed the air in the manner of a large rodent.

"Greetings, my fine friend," Elfloq said softly.

The pink, veined ears of the creature perked up like a cat's. "Who are you?"

"I am Elfloq, a familiar. A recent acquisition of one of the Oligarchs, whom I serve with absolute loyalty and discretion. And who would you be?"

"Faal, lord. I'm a scrovelling. Don't say you've seen me! I don't mean no harm, sir. I'm just looking for a meal. The birds settle at night and if I'm lucky I'll nab one before it gets away."

"Your secret is safe with me, Faal. But I do need your help." Elfloq could see the nervousness, bordering on fear if not actual terror inherent in the quivering shape. "All in the service of the Oligarchs, of course."

Faal bowed. "Anything you desire, sir."

"I'm on a secret mission. I cannot disclose its details. I'm new and I seem to have lost my bearings. I wish to get back inside the Palace, ideally through a door which very few persons know about. If you can help me, the Oligarchs would be delighted to reward you, although that may not be immediate, you understand."

"No, no, please don't mention me! I'll help you. Just pretend you never saw me. Their were-cats hunt us and tear us scrovellings to pieces. I can show you a secret door, but it's locked tight. Not been opened for a long, long time."

Elfloq grinned to himself. "A fair trade. Show me the door and then go your way. I'll not breathe a syllable."

Faal scrambled and scuttled over the desiccated stonework, Elfloq following in the air, not prepared to risk falling through the roof, until, among a remote sequence of tumbled chimneys and walls, Faal found the promised door. Age had warped it, its lintel bowed, and it seemed that it would be impassable, as fixed as the walls around it. Elfloq waved his nervous companion away, and once Faal was well gone, took from his tiny satchel the Key of Keys. Elfloq put its powers to the test, slipping it into the rusted lock. The key's properties morphed it to fit any lock, any size. It was only a matter of moments before Elfloq had the door open. It creaked and shed a mist of rust, but allowed enough room for him to gain egress.

Once inside, Elfloq pushed the door closed, leaving it unlocked in case he needed to retreat hastily later. Although Elfloq's progress was hampered by almost complete darkness, he was able to navigate his way through several narrow passageways, down steps that were thick with dust and through rooms that must have been long out of use. There were two more doors to open, easily enough with the remarkable key, before Elfloq came into a better lit section of the Palace.

He heard voices ahead and advanced cautiously. Two men were disappearing down yet another stairwell, engaged in a loud conversation, their words slurred, suggesting they had been imbibing. Possibly while on duty, as they both wore accoutrements that suggested they were guards or soldiers. They reached the bottom of the stairs and turned aside. Elfloq looked up and saw a void above the corridor, crossed with thick beams – an ideally shadowy space, up to which he flew silently, becoming just another shadow.

He was able to hop along the beams, following the two

guards, and again their voices became clear, though they were now careful to disguise the fact they'd be drinking.

"A four-hour watch," said one of them. "Nothing duller. Who would be foolish enough to attempt to break into the Temple of Hungry Night, even to filch the ruby?"

"A sorcerer might try, but there's enough high magic set up in there to deter an army of thieves. Hardly seems worth having guards on the door. Never mind, Havillius, I've brought the cards."

"The exotic ones?"

Elfloq didn't hear the reply, which was lost in the low chuckles of the two men. Ruby! They were guarding a ruby. It must be *the* ruby. The object of his search.

The men reached a door at the end of the long corridor, where two other guards stood on either side of it. The four of them exchanged pleasantries, before the original two left, their watch over, to be replaced by the newcomers. Elfloq moved around the spaces above the corridor with the utmost delicacy. He had a key that would open this chamber, but how to get the men away from the door, which appeared to be significantly thick, banded with steel and triple locked at the very least. Elfloq was certain he could slip above it, in the rafters, and into the room, but the men would surely notice his passage. Perhaps there'd be a time when the guards would doze off through boredom, at least enough to enable him to attempt an entry.

"The moon's well up," said the guard called Havillius. "Nebucas the Oligarch told me to expect him and his lady guest at about this time. Look lively, Tennius."

Tennius grinned. "The divine Zishti-Aroon? Queen of the Western Palatinate? Word is that Nebucas lusts after her. Well, what man doesn't? But he seems to be making a serious play for her."

"And she'd like a place among the Oligarchs. Though I don't think that's the main thing on her mind. What is it that ladies of her substance and standing enjoy most, aside from power, of course?"

Tennius was laughing softly. "Of course! The ruby. Yet surely she wouldn't dare attempt to purloin it?"

"No," agreed Havillius. "Though she evidently wants to see it. Hence this visit. Hsst. They come!" The two men snapped to attention, apparently primed for any necessary defence of the door.

Elfloq watched as two more figures emerged from the darkness of the corridor. One was a tall man, splendidly robed in white trimmed with bright blue, his dark hair swept back from his forehead and down across his shoulders. His face was carefully made up, his eyes highlighted to give him an exaggerated stare. Beside him, much shorter, was the woman, Zishti-Aroon. As far as Elfloq understood such things, she was a rare beauty, with a full figure and a face whose perfect proportions were marred by a scowl that suggested both extreme hauteur and arrogance. She was used to wielding power, Elfloq knew, and probably without mercy.

"How goes the night?" said the man in a voice that tolled deeply, like a bell.

"Master Nebucas," said Havillius, and both guards bowed. "All is quiet, sire."

"I have some administrative duties to perform," said the Oligarch solemnly. "In the Temple. Be so good as to open the door and escort us within."

Elfloq saw his opportunity, waiting until the door was open and both guards followed the Oligarch and royal lady beyond. Quickly he made his way overhead to the wall of the temple, where, as he suspected there were narrow openings alongside the beams, enough for him to wriggle through. He disturbed an amount of dust in so doing, but not enough to catch the attention of the guards, whose eyes were locked on the Queen of the Western Palatinate, their attention totally snared by her movements. Elfloq slid along another beam, into the chamber and again became very still.

Nebucas dismissed the guards, who went back outside and locked the door. The Oligarch turned to Zishti-Aroon and smiled. They embraced and Elfloq waited impatiently while they kissed and murmured things to one another and went through the various rituals of human courtship to the point at which Elfloq wondered if they were actually going to consummate their lust for each other. Nebucas certainly seemed prepared so to do – Elfloq had seen such behaviour in men many times, lust disguised thinly as love—but Nebucas' partner pushed him gently aside, looking around the chamber. She, too, feigned love, and probably lust as well, Elfloq decided. Any such emotion she felt was not for the man, but for the treasure.

"We don't have much time," she told him. "Show me the ruby! Later we can enjoy ourselves as much as we desire. And when we are wed -"

"Of course, my beautiful one. Here – let me show you." Nebucas took several steps and positioned himself in the centre of a circular mosaic, and whispered a few words into the ether. Elfloq had the ears of a cat, and heard them clearly, memorizing them. He watched as a section of floor rose up, a slender stone column, then unfolded like the petals of a large flower. And there, revealed at its centre, was the ruby. Such a gem! Elfloq stared at its brilliant red glow, almost mesmerized.

Zishti-Aroon rushed forward, though she stopped a pace or two from the prize. "Can I touch it?" she said, her body trembling.

"Very carefully," said the Oligarch. "It is alive. We have yet to learn of all its powers. It is not an easy thing to control. It is, after all, the heart of a god."

The Queen reached out and brushed the ruby with her fingertips. "So cold!" she said, withdrawing her touch. "Yet beautiful beyond words."

"It shall be yours, my wedding gift to you."

They embraced and kissed again, while Elfloq stifled a yawn or two. Fortunately the couple did not stay for long. Nebucas returned the ruby on its column to the place of concealment, then went to the chamber's door and knocked upon it. The guards let him and his lady out.

Elfloq waited for a long time, by which he expected the two men outside to be lulled by their boredom, at the point where their senses had become dulled enough to miss any slight sound the familiar might accidentally make. He dropped down into the chamber, ears cocked for other sounds. If there were guardians here, he'd have to act swiftly to confuse them. He stood in the centre of the mosaic and spoke the words he had memorized. At once the column rose again and the jewel was revealed in all its blushing scarlet. Elfloq studied it briefly, then took the plunge and swept it from its perch, dropping it into the little bag satchel he had unwrapped for the purpose.

Immediately there was a whirring, several loud clicks and a humming sound that suggested a portal had been opened, allowing the egress of a strong wind, which began a low but frightful moaning. The Temple of Hungry Night was about to live up to its name. Elfloq flew upwards, back to the beams, clutching the satchel to him in horror. He peered into the darkness at the far edge of the chamber, from which the unearthly, threatening howls were coming, slowly building up in intensity.

If he had expected to see the ferocious creatures responsible for these sounds emerging and rushing upon him, he was surprised to find that, apart from a strong current of warm, dusty air, nothing actually happened. His eyes pierced the darkness and he allowed himself a grin. The source of the wind's sounds became apparent. There were several tubes and flutes set above the ceiling. It was the passage of a strong gale through these that created the unnerving sounds. They were harmless. They had, however, alerted the guards.

The door creaked open slowly and the two men gazed into the chamber, swords before them, their faces clear evidence of their fear. Elfloq took the opportunity to slip further along the beam and wriggle out above the corridor. Quickly he retraced his steps along the beams, leaving the guards to deal with the Hungry Night and at some point discover that it was little more than a lot of hot air.

Elfloq was soon back out on the roof, locking the secret door behind him. There was no sign of Faal or any of the other beings he had called scrovellings. It had been ridiculously easy, which made him suspicious and doubly cautious. However, there were times when life did other than give him a hefty kick. Possibly this was one of them.

*

Thorgobrund bent over the table, a magnifying lens affixed to his one good eye, and examined at length the array of tiny, glittering jewels spread out before him. He grunted with pleasure, or muttered with annoyance, scowled with uncertainty and chuckled with amusement as he mentally weighed the relative values of the objects. At length he sat back on his teetering stool and gazed at the hunched figure opposite him.

"Most of these are rubbish," he announced. "Not even worth the price of a decent meal."

His guest, whose lugubrious face had melted into an even grimmer mask of sorrow, nodded. "Well, I'll take them away. Perhaps I can trick someone at the market into thinking they're of value." He made to sweep the jewels back into the scruffy pouch in which he had brought them.

"Wait, wait," said Thorgobrund, leaning forward, his lens gleaming, a last ray or two of hope. "I *may* be able to make use of some of them. Of course, I'll have to invest time and effort in selling them on, which reduces their paltry value even more. I don't know -"

"Take them. All I ask is a little to tide me over until I can snatch something far more valuable. And bring it to you, of course."

"I'm a soft-hearted old fool, Slivvardi. Here, take this." The jeweller pushed a small heap of coins across the table. Once the minor thief had gone, Thorgobrund smiled to himself, again studying the jewels. "Nice haul," he whispered. "At least two sea-nymph eyes and I'm sure this is a Green Mindwindow from Elderfingal. Lovely. Six months, a year perhaps, towards my eventual goal and enough to be able to -" His words were cut off as he heard another knock on his door.

"Come in!" he said as he swept the jewels away into a cloth and tucked it inside his voluminous robe. "Ah," he said, recognizing the diminutive figure who had entered his shop. "Elfloq, you have returned. Let me guess – you failed in your avowed task and have come to -"

"Not at all," said the familiar. His batrachian features had moulded themselves into a rare smile. "I have succeeded where nineteen others failed."

Thorgobrund gaped. "Gods of the Starless Heavens, you are jesting! You have purloined the heart of – but no, let's not name the god here. Show me, carefully mind. Kings would lay cities waste for such a jewel."

Elfloq undid his satchel and allowed the jeweller a glance within, to where vivid red light danced like fire.

Thorgobrund sat back, holding his chest as if warding off an attack. "To be honest with you -"

"For once -"

"I did not think you could achieve this. Were you followed?" A new look of horror crossed the jeweller's face, his eye lens dropping into his lap.

"No. I had the means to enter and quit the world of the Palace of Perpetuity, which must remain a secret. All you need to know is – I have the jewel. Take it and test it. I have already told you what I want. Is it ready?"

"Yes, yes, I have worked on it ceaselessly since you came to me. Time was of the absolute essence, you said. You are on a three-day mission, isn't that so?"

"Quite. One more day remains." Elfloq pushed the satchel across the table.

Thorgobrund took it with shaking hands. *Such a prize!* "I am mystified, Elfloq. Why, by all the gods, would you want to exchange this wonderful jewel, whose value and power is inestimable, for a counterfeit version?"

"One day I might tell you. For now, satisfy yourself and give me the jewel you have made for me."

Thorgobrund took from a drawer another small bundle of cloth. Elfloq unwrapped it and studied the facsimile. "Wonderful," he said. "You have excelled yourself."

"Well, my labours will have been well worth it, once I sell the original."

"You have a buyer in mind?" said Elfloq casually.

"I can think of several extraordinarily wealthy princes, a king or two, even an emperor."

"It's financial gain you seek, then?"

"What else is left to me? My eyesight will not last me much longer. As you can see, I have but my one eye left to serve me -"

"What would you give to have your missing eye returned – nay, replaced with a perfect new one? And your entire eyesight restored, better than ever, indefinitely?"

Thorgobrund gaped. "Why, such a thing is not possible -"

"What if I could provide you with a buyer for that ruby who could do all these things for you, as the price for it?"

"You know of such a, a — wizard?"

Elfloq nodded. "Indeed. Give me a little time and I'll have him beating a path to your door."

Soon afterwards, clutching his satchel and the false ruby, Elfloq again took to the astral realm.

*

Aggrabal the Aesthete had chosen a private suite of rooms in yet another run-down, little known establishment, where prying eyes and pricked-up ears, human and otherwise, were unlikely to focus on him. He sat on a barely comfortable divan, cushions strewn about him, and near at hand a tall, obsidian statue loomed over him. It gleamed in the light of several candles as if it had been waxed, its dimensions perfect, its face stern but intelligent.

"So, my little friend," Aggrabal said to Elfloq, who stood before him, clutching a little satchel, something approaching a grin on his face. "Can I take it that you have pulled off the trick? You have actually pilfered the ruby, the heart of Uzbandazra?"

"Indeed I have, master," Elfloq said with a bow.

"And well within the three days. Show me!"

Elfloq undid the straps of the satchel, reached inside it and pulled out the glowing ember that was the ruby. Aggrabal gasped aloud and leaned forward, his fingers curling and uncurling, like a huge hawk eager to grip its next meal. Elfloq handed it over.

The trader shuddered as he took the gem, which sat neatly in the palm of one hand. He shuddered, his eyes closing in rapture. "Such a marvel," he said. "You have done well, familiar."

Elfloq took the Key of Keys from his belt and held it up. "According to our bargain, I have almost a day left in which to use this. After that, it will make its way back to you."

Aggrabal could scarcely tear his attention from the jewel. "What? Oh, yes, of course. Use it wisely, and as many times as you like. But as you say, after three days, it will find its way back to me. It has that power. Someone, or something, will return it to me. I strongly urge you not to resist its efforts."

Elfloq inclined his head.

Aggrabal stood and went to the statue. "And now, for the completion of my reconstruction! Uzbandazra will live again!" Without further ado, he offered the ruby to the statue, touching its brilliant surface to the chest of the god's image.

Elfloq watched – with more than a little relief – as the ruby was slowly absorbed into the statue at precisely the place where the god's heart should be. Shortly it had disappeared and Aggrabal stepped back, eyes closed, arms open wide as if about to welcome the embrace of the god. The statue moved, a grinding sound emanating from it like stone on stone. Its legs came free of the low pedestal and – it walked! It raised its arms and took Aggrabal in its embrace.

The trader let out a single shout of joy and Elfloq hopped back, watching the remarkable transformation. Aggrabal and the statue were *merging* into one. The trader's clothes fell to the floor, leaving him naked save for a simple breechclout. His skin had become the obsidian colour of the god, though his features remained the same. Elfloq felt a sudden rush of terror. This was something he had not contemplated.

Aggrabal and Uzbandazra were one and the same. The god had merely been imprisoned in human guise. It had restored itself. Or so it might have thought.

Elfloq watched the face of the reconstructed god, its wide smile, its shudders of ecstasy at being reborn. This wasn't supposed to happen. Not with a false heart -

However, Aggrabal's face abruptly contorted into a frightful grimace, a look of tortured agony and he bent over double, clutching at his chest.

"What...what is happening? What have you done?" he snarled at Elfloq, hands reaching out, though he had dropped to his knees, the pain coursing through him so terrible that his movements were curtailed. He crashed to the floor, crawling across it like a damaged insect.

"It is a temporary difficulty, master," said Elfloq, relieved to see that the maimed god couldn't possibly grab hold of him and administer any kind of revenge. Indeed, the god was rendered helpless as a babe in arms.

"The ruby! It is not the true heart -"

"That is so. Yet you may rest assured that I have taken it from its recent place of safe keeping and passed it on. I know exactly where it is."

"Then fetch it! Bring it to me!"

"Can I suggest an alternative, master? One that will satisfy us both, and one other."

Aggrabal fought the pain, which appeared to be getting considerably worse. He nodded, his face straining with effort. Abruptly something slid out of his chest, and the false ruby dropped to the floor, its light dimming.

"I will give you the name and the whereabouts of the new owner of the ruby. The real one, that is. In exchange, I want to keep the Key of Keys. Lift the three-day spell and let the key be mine hereafter."

Aggrabal struggled to stand, tears streaming down his cheeks. "This is nothing less than thievery! You deceived me. That is reprehensible. You deserve to be -"

"Do you want the ruby?"

"Curse you, yes."

"Then I will impart the information. Promise me that you will make the key mine."

Aggrabal sighed. "Very well. I do so promise." He muttered a series of spells and cantillations, weaving the air with his hands. "There! It is done. The accursed key is yours."

"And you will not pursue me?"

"I will not."

"You will not attempt to punish me, or otherwise cause me to suffer as a result of this bargain?"

Aggrabal growled, but nodded. "I will not." Again he sealed his words with the appropriate sorcery.

"Thank you, master." Elfloq pocketed the Key of Keys. "The man you seek is Thorgobrund, the jeweller. He will sell you the ruby. To you, his price will be a small thing. No blame attaches to him for this exchange of ours."

"Thorgobrund? Yes, I have heard of him, though he dwells in a somewhat remote realm. I will seek him out at once. I sincerely hope that you and I shall not meet again."

"Of course, master. But as the restored god, you will have

216

far more important matters to attend to than a mere flea such as I."

Aggrabal raised himself to his full height. "Well, quite. It is time I again took my place among the higher beings."

*

Elfloq slipped on to the astral realm and flitted to and fro for a short time. He felt pleased with himself. It had been an unnerving experience, cheating the god, but doubtless Uzbandazra would quickly forget him and, well, a god wouldn't need a Key of Keys. For the moment, Elfloq decided to slip on to one of the quieter places he knew, a grey realm not only lacking in colour, but also in activity of any note, where a thin populace was spread over several bleak continents. In the small city state of Burra Barga, he found an inn, the last building before the desert, and secreted himself in a dusty corner where no one paid him the slightest heed.

It took the familiar a while to pluck up the courage, but at last he pulled out the key. It had the look of any normal key, its metal dull, slightly rusted, its shape common enough. He would test its veracity. Where to choose? He could think of any number of realms he was not able to visit under normal circumstances, most of them guarded either by frightful monsters or devastating spells. Where would his master be? If he were to be on one such terrifying world, Elfloq could reunite with him, knowing he would be safe under his shadow. Yet if he chose the wrong world -

"You appear to be wrestling with a dilemma," said a deep voice close by.

Elfloq jumped as if he had been thrown a hissing snake, almost dropping the key. He fumbled with it, getting it into a pocket before meeting the gaze of the tall being who now materialized in front of him. It...

"Darquementi!" Elfloq said, with a gasp. New terrors started to wriggle around inside him like angry wasps.

The Divine Asker, for it was indeed he, bowed. His stern gaze fixed the diminutive familiar as it attempted to slide under the table, doubtless to attempt flight back to the astral. Darquementi would not allow that.

"And what bauble have you prized from a victim's fingers this time?"

"A trifle, great lord. Passing dust. A mere gewgaw."

"You are far too modest. Show me."

Elfloq felt his bowels turning to water. He fumbled again and set the Key of Keys on the table. Darquementi leaned forward, studied it for a moment and nodded. Elfloq wondered if it would be enough for the Asker, and he might, just possibly think nothing of it. After all, it *looked* like any ordinary key, did it not? Cautiously he made to slide it back towards him.

Darquementi shook his cowled head. "That key fell into the wrong hands some while ago. The minor god who stole it has kept it well hidden from its proper guardians for a long time. I won't ask you how in all the Pits of the Abyss you obtained such an object, Elfloq, but know this much – I am grateful." One elongated hand reached out, unfurled a bony finger and prodded the key.

Elfloq watched as the Asker slid it across the table, then picked it up. "Oh, and you have had its spell removed! However did you manage that? No – don't tell me. Spare yourself the embarrassment."

As the Key of Keys disappeared into the scarlet robes, lost forever to his sight, Elfloq knew, the familiar thought better of fabricated a tale of how he had always intended to restore it to its rightful owners. Discretion, he decided, was the better part of valour.

"The key has many wonderful properties, Elfloq. It gives so much freedom to those who possess it. Yet there are so many dangers attached to it. You are well rid of it.

"For a familiar, especially one without a master, you are most fortunate. You enjoy unprecedented freedom yourself. Not only to roam about the astral and the many dimensions it opens on to, but you have a certain intellectual freedom, freedom to express yourself in a diverse company, and be tolerant of views you do not yourself hold, to speak nothing of the freedom of choice of gods, tenets, companions, the arts. Go out and relish that freedom. It is beyond price."

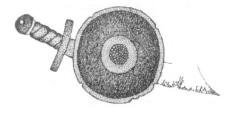

ALSO AVAILABLE FROM
PARALLEL UNIVERSE PUBLICATIONS

Carl Barker: *Parlour Tricks*
Charles Black: *Black Ceremonies*
Benjamin Blake: *Standing on the Threshold of Madness*
Mike Chinn: *Radix Omnium Malum*
Ezeiyoke Chukwunonso: *The Haunted Grave & Other Stories*
Irvin S. Cobb: *Fishhead: The Darker Tales of Irvin S. Cobb*
Adrian Cole: *Tough Guys*
Andrew Darlington: *A Saucerful of Secrets*
Kate Farrell: *And Nobody Lived Happily Ever After*
Craig Herbertson: *The Heaven Maker & Other Gruesome Tales*
Craig Herbertson: *Christmas in the Workhouse*
Erik Hofstatter: *The Crabian Heart*
Andrew Jennings: *Into the Dark*
David Ludford: *A Place of Skulls & Other Tales*
Johnny Mains: *A Little Light Screaming*
Johnny Mains: *A Distasteful Horror Story*
Jessica Palmer: *Other Visions of Heaven and Hell*
Jessica Palmer: *Fractious Fairy Tales*
Jim Pitts: *The Fantastical Art of Jim Pitts*
David A. Riley: *Goblin Mire*
David A. Riley: *Their Cramped Dark World & Other Tales*
David A. Riley: *His Own Mad Demons*
David A. Riley: *Moloch's Children*
David A. Riley: *After Nightfall & Other Weird Tales*
Joseph Rubas: *Shades: Dark Tales of Supernatural Horror*
Eric Ian Steele: *Nightscape*
David Williamson: *The Chameleon Man & Other Terrors*

https://paralleluniversepublications.blogspot.com/

Printed in Great Britain
by Amazon